He found himself touching warm, soft female skin...

What?

Oh, she smelled good.

Jackson eased closer. The curving line of her shoulder captivated him. He couldn't resist—he put his lips where her shoulder met her throat. A pulse beat there, slow and steady. His hand moved downward to capture her breast.

And then she made a sound like a purr and turned to him.

He raised his head to look at her more carefully in the darkness of the hotel room and at the same time she opened her eyes.

His heart stopped. Her eyes opened wide.

Holy hell...

He knew this woman's name perfectly. And most of the time wished he didn't.

What was Lauren doing in his bed?

Dear Reader,

If you've been to the famous Hotel del Coronado near San Diego, then Hotel Messina might seem a little familiar. I love that part of the world. When I dreamed up my latest Harlequin Blaze I was living in Southern California, so it was natural to incorporate my favorite places, including Napa and San Francisco.

When I thought about plot, I drew on the best plotter of them all, Shakespeare. This is my riff on *Much Ado About Nothing*, with the cynical couple who banter and snipe at each other, but are deep down crazy about each other, and the second couple, the ones who are in love with their ideal vision of love, but the minute the going gets tough they start to fall apart. Naturally, this is a modern and much sexier tale, but I owe William for the initial inspiration.

As always, I love to hear from readers. Please come visit me on the web at nancywarren.net.

Happy Reading!

Nancy Warren

USA TODAY BESTSELLING AUTHOR

Nancy Warren

Best Man...with Benefits

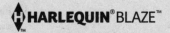

Recycling programs
for this product may
not exist in your area.

ISBN-13: 978-0-373-79858-2

Best Man...with Benefits

Printed in U.S.A.

USA TODAY bestselling author **Nancy Warren** lives in the Pacific Northwest, where her hobbies include skiing, hiking and snowshoeing. She's the author of more than forty books and novellas for Harlequin and has won several awards. Visit her website at nancywarren.net.

Books by Nancy Warren

HARLEQUIN BLAZE
Indulge
French Kissing
Under the Influence
Power Play
Too Hot to Handle
My Fake Fiancée
The Ex Factor
Face-Off
Just One Night

Last Bachelor Standing

Game On
Breakaway
Final Score

To get the inside scoop on Harlequin Blaze and its talented writers, be sure to check out blazeauthors.com.

All backlist available in ebook format.

Visit the Author Profile page at Harlequin.com for more titles.

For Elizabeth Jennings and
the Matera Brainstormers.

1

QUESTION: How DO you know when someone is truly your best friend? *Answer:* you love her enough to put up with her semi-douchy fiancé and his completely douchy best buddy.

Asked and answered, Lauren Sanger thought, as she sat on a private patio of Hotel Messina, the swish resort located on a small island off the California coast where, in a few hours, she'd be maid of honor in her best friend's wedding.

Built at the turn of the century, Hotel Messina had housed royalty and A-list celebrities, and been the setting for movies and thousands of weddings.

Amy Ruehl had dreamed of getting married here since she and Lauren had first seen the hotel in a movie back when they were kids. Her parents could afford the outrageous expense, and all the guests had made the trek over to spend the night, celebrate Amy and Seth's wedding, and then go back to their much more mundane lives.

Or maybe that was just Lauren.

The wedding would take place at four in the afternoon. That's what it said on the thick vellum invitations, and with the military precision with which the wedding planner and hotel staff had worked this thing, that's precisely when the ceremony would begin.

It was two now, and the bride and her maid of honor were taking a late lunch break. Their hair was done, makeup awaiting final touches, and their dresses were pressed and neatly hanging.

She and Amy already wore their fancy underwear beneath the thick hotel robes with the gold M logo on the breast pockets.

While they munched on salad and cold cuts and sipped wine, they enjoyed a spectacular view of the white sand beaches and summer blue water that surrounded the hotel. The weather was perfect. A June day without a cloud in the sky and waves that seemed to laugh as they hit the beach.

"Are you nervous?" she asked her best friend. They'd talked about their weddings a lot when they were young. Amy was a firm believer in fairy tales and happy endings. Lauren not so much, but she couldn't be happier that her BFF's dream was about to come true. Seth wouldn't have been her choice, but Amy was crazy about him and that was all that mattered to Lauren.

Amy shook her head, a smile of pure happiness on her face. She always took everything in stride and didn't worry much about the future. Lauren wondered what it would be like to be such an optimist and was fairly certain she'd never know.

"Seth is the man I've waited my whole life for," Amy said. Her voice trembled ever so slightly as she added, "I love him so much."

"No messing up the makeup," Lauren warned, leaning forward to pat her friend's hand.

Amy blinked rapidly, dispelling the momentary wetness. "My only wish is that my best friend and Seth's best friend could like each other, at least a little bit."

Not even for her best friend would she lie and feign any affection for Jackson Monaghan. All she said was, "Hey, we both love you guys. That's all that matters."

"But we're going to be seeing you two all the time. You're the first people we'll have for dinner in our new place, you'll be the godmother of our first child, obviously, and Jackson will be the god—"

"You're pregnant?" Lauren's voice rose. How had she never suspected?

Amy waved a freshly manicured hand in front of her face. "No. I'm just saying."

"Stop planning so far ahead." She put a hand to her chest. "And stop freaking me out."

Amy's face suddenly took on an expression that Lauren would call fatuous if Amy wasn't her best friend. She only wore that expression for one person.

She followed the bride's gaze and, sure enough, two men came into view on the sand below them. Seth, the groom, and Jackson, the best man.

Clearly, the routine for the men of a wedding party was a lot more lax than for the women. The guys were walking barefoot in the sand, wearing their board shorts and sunglasses. They'd ditched their shirts.

She could picture the pair of them scrambling to get dressed fifteen minutes before the ceremony started.

They were a nice-looking pair, she'd give them that.

Seth was a little on the chunky side. He'd been a football player in college and working a desk job, he'd gone a bit to seed. Jackson, on the other hand, was pretty drool-worthy, she had to admit. He sported the torso of an athlete—no doubt, the result of regular workout sessions with a personal trainer at a fancy gym somewhere. He had the permanent five-o'clock shadow of a jaded rock star. His eyes were an Irish blue; his hair a tousled brown that she suspected was salon-highlighted. Everything about him annoyed her.

She scratched her arm. That's what Jackson was like, she thought. Like an itch. The more she tried to get rid of him, the more he irritated her.

"Why don't you like Jackson?" Amy broke into her thoughts. "Every woman I know is crazy about him."

And that was one more thing that irritated her about Jackson Monaghan. He strutted around as if he was God's gift, and the sad part was plenty of women were apparently foolish enough to buy in to the ridiculous notion.

"Honestly, I don't know," she said. "I guess it's a chemistry thing."

Amy sighed, finished her wine. "Well," she said, "I'm going to do everything I can to get you two to like each other."

Oh, goodie.

JACKSON MONAGHAN LOVED the feel of sun on his skin and sand beneath his feet. Wearing a monkey suit and being in a wedding party, not so much.

But, for the guy who'd pretty much saved his life, there wasn't much he wouldn't do.

He and Seth went way back. When Jackson had lost his folks, his grandparents hadn't known what to do with a grieving twelve-year-old. They'd packed him up and sent him to boarding school.

He'd never been exposed to rich people. Didn't know shit about life in a dorm, and the other boys had sensed weakness the way sharks smell blood.

He had been scrawny back then. Sensitive. He'd thought nothing could be worse than losing his parents to a car wreck. He was wrong.

Those first few weeks of boarding school were brutal. Until Seth stepped up. Seth was the kind of kid the other boys respected. He was big, tough, not so good at school but great at sports. From Seth, Jackson had learned how to be one of the boys. And he'd learned how to fight back.

So, if Seth wanted him to show up in a tux and pass a couple of rings to a minister and make a speech, he was down.

He wasn't sure Seth had made the best choice in brides, but his buddy was clearly convinced that Amy was an angel and he wasn't one to make waves. The fiancée's best friend, though?

Ouch. Lauren Sanger was hot, no question. But that mouth that looked as though it had been designed to kiss sweetly and talk dirty mostly hurled insults. At him.

"In a couple of hours, I'll be a married man," Seth suddenly said.

"Yep."

"I always knew I'd get married, have some kids— it's what a man does. But now that it's here, I can't believe it."

"I can't believe you're getting married, either." Everything was going to change. The beers after work, the weekly squash games, the poker games that lasted all night, the Sunday afternoons spent tossing a football around in the park, the snap decisions to fly across the country to watch a hockey or a football game. All that would be over.

"Nothing's going to change," Seth said, sounding almost desperate.

"Of course, nothing will change," Jackson assured him, knowing that nothing would ever be the same.

"Amy's the best thing that ever happened to me," Seth announced. He'd taken to gushing sentiments like this, and Jackson never knew what the correct response was. Usually he said something like, "That's great."

"That's great," he said now.

Seth stooped to pick up a smooth, round pebble. He turned and tried to skim it across the waves, but the pebble bounced once and sank.

"I just wish you and Lauren could get along."

"Probably never going to happen."

"What's the deal with you two, anyway? She's gorgeous, smart, funny."

"I don't know. Some kind of weird chemistry thing." He'd thought *gorgeous*, *smart* and *funny*, too, the first time he'd met Lauren. But from that first conversation on, they'd pretty much disagreed on everything. She seemed to spare no effort to get up his nose. And, being a scrapper with a lot of Irish in him, he gave it right back to her.

Desperate to change the subject, he said, "But Amy's great."

That got them off the tricky subject of Lauren and they passed the rest of their time talking about Amy and Seth's plans for the future. Seth had gone to work for his family's real estate firm and Amy came from money, so it wasn't as if their future was uncertain.

Not like his. With his brains and his education in software design, he'd been recruited by all the big firms, but he'd chosen to throw in his lot with a start-up. He'd liked that they were involved in clean energy, harvesting wind and wave power. Jackson didn't have any money. His grandparents had spent what little money his folks had left on that boarding school and given him what was left to pay for university. With no money to invest, he relied on his own hard work. Going for the start-up over the sure thing was the Irish in him asserting itself again, he thought. He preferred the gamble, where he could seriously make a difference to a company's future, to being just another software engineer at a global social networking company.

He and Seth returned to the hotel with barely enough time to shower and change.

The bride and groom had opted for a garden wedding with a ballroom booked as a bad weather backup, but one look at the sky told Jackson that no backup plan would be needed. Seth and Amy were probably the luckiest couple he'd ever known. Nothing ever went wrong for either of them. They were loved, pampered, rich and nauseatingly happy with each other. Of course there wouldn't be a cloud in the sky on their wedding day.

Jackson took a final glance in the full-length mirror in his hotel room before heading out. His tie was straight, fly done up. Rings in one pocket, speech in another. He was good to go.

His room was on the third floor where most of the bridal party and a few of the guests were staying. The bride and groom were spending their wedding night in the penthouse bridal suite and the remainder of the guests were scattered throughout the hotel.

Seth knocked on his door and he opened it. "Ready to do this thing?"

"Yeah."

"Okay." And they strode off down the hall.

The wedding planner had given them a staging area in the lobby, and they showed up with a minute or two to spare. The woman standing there with a headset and a clipboard wasn't the main planner. She was some kind of assistant. She checked them out, stepped forward and straightened Seth's tie. "You have the rings?" she asked Jackson, and he nodded.

She spoke into a headset. "I have the groom and best man ready to go."

They stood around for a few minutes like soldiers waiting to go into battle. It would have been less nerve-racking if there were more guys in the platoon than just him and Seth. But for all that she'd wanted a fancy wedding, Amy had insisted she only wanted Lauren to stand up for her. Which meant Seth only got a best man. No groomsmen.

The assistant pulled out two florist's boxes, and he was forced to stand there while she attached a white rose boutonniere to his jacket. The smell of roses always reminded him of the only funeral he'd ever attended. He hated that smell.

"And you're cleared to go," the young woman said to them, as though they were a pair of jets on a runway.

"Good luck, buddy," he said.

Seth turned and gave him an awkward hug. They

slapped each other on the back, and then they made their way out to the wedding venue.

The garden looked like something out of a cheesy movie he would never watch. Something with Hugh Grant in it and a load of English accents. There were flowers everywhere—on a rose arbor that he and Seth had to walk under, on the chairs lined up precisely on the lawn where the guests were already seated, and all over the gazebo where the ceremony would take place. A harp was playing softly.

The guests were dressed so well, some of the women in hats, that he barely recognized anyone.

He trod down the aisle and paused, as they'd rehearsed, in front of the minister, who consulted a book so earnestly it looked as though he was refreshing himself on the words of the marriage ceremony.

Behind him, he heard shuffling and low conversation. Somebody was sniffling. Crying already? Or allergies? he wondered idly.

After a minute or two, the intro to "Here Comes the Bride" started up. He knew the piece had a real name, but he only ever heard it played at weddings.

He and Seth both turned, as did every person in the audience.

Lauren started walking up the aisle.

He might find spending time with her as fun as, say, stumbling into a hive of hornets and escaping only to land in a field of poison ivy, but he had to admit she looked good.

Gorgeous, even.

Her dress was a pale green that left her shoulders bare. He'd never really noticed what nice curves the woman had or that her legs were spectacular.

She wore her dark hair piled high and whoever had done her makeup had highlighted her big, dark eyes and colored her lips so they looked plump and kissable.

As though she felt his gaze on her, Lauren looked his way and he felt sucker punched.

Quickly, he averted his gaze but not before he'd seen her eyes widen and felt a completely unexpected and absolutely unwanted stab of lust.

That was the trouble with weddings, he'd always thought. They made a person act like a fool. People were forever hooking up at weddings with girls they wouldn't be caught dead with normally.

He wasn't going there.

Even as his breath caught in his throat, he assured himself he wasn't going there.

2

LAUREN WENT THROUGH the motions of being the perfect maid of honor. She took the bouquet from Amy when it was time for her and Seth to exchange rings. Helped her adjust her dress after she and Seth had kissed and they were officially married, then fell in behind the beaming bride and groom with Jackson by her side.

There was an invisible force field between her and the best man. They couldn't stand each other, so what had that strange moment been about when he'd stared at her as though he'd never seen her before and she'd felt for a second as though she couldn't breathe?

No doubt he'd seen as much crazy hooking up at weddings as she had. Or maybe he was one of those guys who thought bridesmaids always wanted sex.

She'd rather have sex with—well, she couldn't think of anybody she'd rather have sex with right at the moment, but the point was she didn't want to have sex with Jackson Monaghan.

Although, looking around the crowd at the number of women checking him out, she seemed to be the only single woman who didn't.

They were stuck side by side in the receiving line, and she shook hands and kissed cheeks and smiled politely as guests passed by on the way to congratulate the bride and groom. A woman named Cynthia who had gone to school with her and Amy held on to Jackson's hand a little too long. "You look so good in a tux," she gushed. Then, still holding his hand, she turned to Lauren. "Doesn't he? Doesn't he look good in a tux?"

"Yes. He looks like you could slip him a twenty and get seated at the best table in the house."

"Oh, I know exactly where I'd seat you," he said to her, his eyes narrowing.

Cynthia giggled awkwardly and moved on.

She blinked her eyes. "Not the best table? What would that take? Fifty bucks?"

He squinted his eyes like a gunslinger at high noon. "We could work together. In that dress you look like the cigarette girl at the bar in *Mad Men*."

There was a break in the stream of guests coming down the receiving line. Amy turned to her and said, "How are you holding up?"

"Fine. Except Jackson thinks I look like the cigarette girl at the bar in *Mad Men*."

Amy's eyes grew wide. "That's so weird. That's exactly what you said when you first tried on the dress."

It was one thing to say it about yourself, and another thing to have a guy say it about you. But Amy had already turned to greet the next guest who stopped before her.

The wedding was designed so that guests could enjoy drinks and appetizers outside while the wedding party had their photos taken and then move inside for dinner and dancing later.

Amy was so happy it was impossible not to feel happy for her and an equally elated Seth, pleased everything had worked out for them and hopeful for their future.

The wedding party spent an hour with a professional photographer who had the easiest job in the world since the location was nothing but one big photo op and Seth and Amy were two blissful, attractive people.

But Gunter, the photographer, was German and a perfectionist. He took ages setting up each shot, ordering his assistant to move Amy's bouquet slightly to the left, waiting for the slight breeze to drop before snapping a photo of the newlyweds.

Then he brought Jackson and Lauren into the photos. They stood stiffly side by side, not touching. Gunter stared through his viewfinder, shook his head, muttered, *"Nein,"* and then muttered some more in German. He stepped forward and placed Lauren's bouquet in her right hand and took her left. He picked up Jackson's right hand and posed his arm so that Lauren rested her left wrist over his, her palm resting on the back of his right hand. Gunter then turned the two of them so they angled toward the bridal couple, which put her body up against the best man's.

She felt ridiculous and awkward with the warmth of his arm beneath hers and the feel of his hand under her palm. She felt the rigid hardness in him that was probably a combination of muscle tone and the same tension she felt.

"Smile like this is the happiest day of your life," Gunter instructed them.

"I'm not that good an actress," she muttered before pulling out a fake smile for the camera.

Amy suddenly turned, breaking the stiff pose. "Isn't this fun?" she cried. "Can you imagine anything better?"

"Being trapped in an airless glass tank crawling with tarantulas?" Jackson said softly.

"Swimming with sharks while bleeding from an artery?" Lauren said.

"Plunging to earth right after the parachute doesn't open?" he countered.

She was so glad when the photo session was over and they were released to join the party.

Even though Amy and her mother had tried to keep the numbers down, there were well over a hundred guests. Including the frat boys, as she and Amy called Seth's school friends.

The frat boys had all grown up together in a fancy boarding school, and as far as Lauren could tell, they'd never outgrown their schoolboy pranks.

If Amy and Seth walked into the bridal suite and found a naked porn star reclining on the bed, or a copy of *Sex for Dummies* on Seth's pillow, she wouldn't be surprised.

She wandered among the guests, chatting to those she knew, making small talk with strangers. Her index finger throbbed from where she'd burned it last night. She'd stayed up late finishing her wedding gift for Amy and Seth. She was a stained-glass artisan and she'd completed a tricky window for the townhouse Amy and Seth had bought in downtown San Francisco with some generous financing from their parents.

She hoped Amy liked the piece. It was one she was really proud of. She fished an ice cube from the glass of ice water she was drinking and held it to her sore finger.

"What happened to your hand?"

She hadn't even noticed Jackson come up beside her. "I burned it."

She waited for some smart-ass comment, but he actually looked like a human being for a second. "Ouch."

They both looked down at her hand. Her nails were short, and with her line of work, she almost never painted them so it was strange to see them perfectly manicured in pale pink. "Occupational hazard."

"I thought you worked in a winery."

She glanced up, surprised that he knew even that much about her. He seemed a bit embarrassed himself. "Seth mentioned it," he said.

"I do. Leonato Estate Winery funds my real work, designing and making stained glass. Not a high-paying profession." She dropped the ice cube back into her drink with a plop. It was true. She loved what she did. Had found her calling when she'd traveled to Europe after college. She and Amy had gone together, and as much as she'd enjoyed seeing the Louvre and the Eiffel Tower and the Colosseum, it was the churches and cathedrals with their stained glass that had transfixed her. Venice and its glass makers had inspired her to change her career plans from a vague notion of getting a business degree to studying the ancient art of stained-glass work with an eye to making it look modern.

She was doing okay for an artisan. She sold her work through a couple of galleries and high-end craft markets and a few architects called her from time to time. Maybe she wasn't getting rich, but she was managing. In a couple of years, if her sales continued to increase, she'd be able to quit the winery and work on her glass full-time.

"Amy's mom sent me to find you. Dinner's about to start."

"Oh. Right."

They entered the ballroom together into a sea of tables. The surfaces of the tables were crowded with the printed wedding programs, place cards and specially made chocolates wrapped in foil the same color as Lauren's dress.

Naturally, she and Jackson were seated at the head table with Amy and Seth and both sets of parents.

Her place card put her between the two douches.

She knew exactly what food would be served and which wines, just as she'd known the foiled candies would match her dress. Because Amy had discussed every detail with her.

Even if she'd been bored by the details, she had to admit that Amy had been right. All her planning was paying off. From the wafer-thin slices of smoked salmon and capers, to the main meal (a choice of beef Wellington, chicken in a champagne sauce or a vegetarian plate) everything was perfect. From her perch at the head table, Lauren could see that everyone was having a wonderful time.

The frat boys acknowledged the solemnity of the occasion by banging on their wineglasses with their cutlery until Amy and Seth kissed.

"If I ever get married, I'm eloping," she muttered.

She didn't realize she'd been heard until Jackson said, "Me, too."

The frat boys made Amy and Seth kiss a few more times throughout the meal until, finally, it was time for the speeches. To her surprise, Jackson's toast to the bride was both intelligent and funny. Seth's toast to the maid of honor was more about himself and how lucky he was that Amy's best friend liked him, to which Lauren gave a good-natured two-thumbs-up, hoping that thumb-raising didn't constitute actual lying.

Just when it seemed that the formal part of the evening was ending, the frat boys started banging away on their glasses again. Really, those servers needed to take their spoons away and send them to their rooms.

Amy and Seth rose, and Willy, whom she'd nicknamed Head Frat Boy, yelled, "Everybody at the head table. Let's see some kissing."

There was a moment of stunned silence.

"Oh, no," she said.

At the same moment, Jackson muttered, "I don't think so," but as the sound of cutlery on glassware increased, the two sets of parents struggled to their feet. She and Jackson both remained seated until Amy and Seth laughed down at them, Amy saying, "Come on, you guys," and Lauren realized they'd only appear more foolish refusing to play along.

"I am so eloping," she said as she rose reluctantly to her feet.

"Me, too," Jackson agreed. "Let's get this over with," he added, in the tone he'd probably have used on his way to a firing squad.

And then he kissed her.

Glasses clinked and wolves whistled and wedding guests clapped and cheered.

And she felt his mouth on hers. Warm. Not icky at all, in fact, but kind of nice. It was pretty much the briefest possible press of closed lips to closed lips, but still, there was a tiny buzz of something that snapped back and forth between them.

She sat back down as quickly as she could, banging her butt on the chair.

A couple of dances, she said to herself, *circulate, make more small talk, and then I can go to bed*. She'd been up way too late working, and then Amy had called her way too early this morning to remind her to bring a bathing suit. "Because we are going to hit the spa."

Lauren had no idea when they were going to squeeze in time at the spa, but she'd thrown her bathing suit in her suitcase anyway and, giving up on any more sleep, padded to her tiny kitchen to brew coffee.

The short night and long day were catching up with her now. One of the perks of her position of maid of honor was that Amy's parents had insisted on paying for her room. She had a lovely room on the third floor overlooking the ocean. It was dominated by a big, decadent bed, where she could sleep as long as she wanted.

Hotel Messina was the kind of hotel that contained a sprung dance floor at one end of the ballroom and a stage large enough for a big band. In its heyday the hotel had boasted its own band and the rich and famous had waltzed and fox-trotted many a night away here. The French doors were all open to the breeze when the orchestra struck up, and the MC called out the wedding couple for their first dance.

"Hope I don't fall off my heels," Amy said as she walked behind Lauren and giggled.

"You'll be fine," she whispered back.

Maybe it was corny and sentimental, but she had a moment, watching her best friend dance with her brand-new husband. They held each other briefly and then began to move with the music they'd chosen. She'd tried to talk Amy out of it, but ever since she'd seen Kate Winslet and Leonardo DiCaprio on the prow of the *Titanic* she'd been determined that "My Heart Will Go On" would be her wedding song. Lauren had assumed she'd grow out of that idea, but no. And yet, as she watched her best friend in the arms of her new husband, waltzing to Celine Dion, she felt a real hope that they'd be this happy forever.

"And now, would the parents join Mr. and Mrs. Beauregard, please. And the maid of honor and the best man," the rich voice said into the mic.

Oh, crap. This was the part she'd dreaded.

Jackson looked as thrilled as she was as he led the way to the dance floor. They didn't touch until they were pretty much forced to.

He put a hand on her waist.

She put a hand on his shoulder.

He took her other hand. "Ready?"

"I'll fantasize I'm having electric-shock therapy. The time will pass."

He moved her in a circle. "I'll pretend I'm having a last cigarette before the firing squad. I'll enjoy it."

"You smoke?" Gross.

"No. But I think if I knew my life was going to end in a couple of minutes anyway, I might take it up." He twirled her around Seth's parents. "I'd ask for a king-size cigarette. No filter."

She watched Amy and Seth, holding each other so close he kept stepping on her dress. "Think they'll make it?" she asked.

She felt him shrug as his shoulder rose up and down under her hand. "They've got a fifty-fifty chance, statistically."

ACROSS THE ROOM, a table of men who'd all gone to boarding school with Seth and Jackson were making full use of the open bar. They'd moved on from the dinner wine and were now doing shooters.

"Would you do her?" Willy Ragan asked in a general way, his gaze semi-focused on the dance floor.

"Amy?" Rip Sherken asked.

"No. She's married, asshole. The other one."

"The bridesmaid?"

"Yeah."

They all studied Lauren.

"She's hot." Rip burped politely behind his hand. "Bet she goes for Jackson. They always go for Jackson."

"Not her. Haven't you noticed? She hates him. Look at them. Acting like a couple of brooms dancing."

Rip snorted. "The chicks are always all over Jackson. And he gets stuck with the one woman who thinks he's dog meat. Excellent."

And between that shooter and the next, Willy came up with a plan that was way funnier than their original idea to TP the bridal suite.

Willy outlined his plan rapidly while all his buddies concentrated on the details.

"How you gonna get her room key?" Rip wanted to know.

"It's probably in her purse, which she left on her seat," Willy said. "I saw her leave. Her room's just down from mine, so I know which one it is."

Tricking the maid of honor and the best man, who hated each other, into sharing the same hotel room was, they agreed, way better than their original plan.

Though, if there was time for both, they still planned to toilet paper the suite.

"We better get her key now, while they're all dancing," Willy said.

He got up and found Lauren's clutch purse on her chair as he'd expected. The clasp took his thick fingers a second to work out, but he soon had it open. There was nothing in there but a couple of tissues, some lipstick and her room key.

He pocketed the room key and then, while he was standing, realized he needed to pee. He veered off to take care of business while he mentally perfected the details of the plan. They weren't too complicated. Mostly, the plan involved getting Jackson drunk.

LAUREN ENDED UP having a lot more fun at the reception than she thought she would. A couple of single guys hit on her, as did one older, very drunk, and very married friend of Amy's father. She laughed with Amy and her girlfriends and, when Amy threw the bouquet, made certain to stand way out of the line of fire.

Then Amy and Seth headed off up the bridal suite and her duties were over.

Still, she hung around for another half an hour or so before slipping away. That luxurious room with the huge bed and the balcony looking out to the sea beckoned her.

Her supposed escort, the best man, had abandoned his tuxedo jacket a while ago and sat hunched around a table with the rest of the frat boys where the booze was flowing. A couple of women had drifted over, and she suspected there'd be some pairing up when the night finally ended. Cynthia was sitting next to Jackson, she noted, hanging on every word he said. Pathetic.

She found her clutch, which had somehow fallen to the floor, and slipped out of the emptying ballroom. Before she got to the elevator, she dug in her purse for her key card, but it wasn't there.

Shaking her head at her own foolishness, she went to the front desk, where they gave her another.

With a sleepy thanks, she headed up to bed.

When she entered her luxurious hotel room, she threw open the balcony doors and watched the ocean for a few minutes. The moon gilded the waves and the sand stretched endlessly in either direction. A couple, guests of the hotel, probably, walked on the beach. They seemed happily in love. *Good for them*, she thought, as she went back inside and brushed her teeth. She donned the pretty nightgown she'd brought with her and stretched out in the huge, decadent bed.

She imagined Amy and Seth were right this moment enjoying married sex up in the bridal suite, and that was her last thought before she fell into exhausted sleep.

JACKSON PULLED OFF his tie and settled around the table with his buddies. He'd done his part, made a speech, danced with the ice queen herself, and now he could simply hang out. He passed on the shooters, but he accepted a scotch. He felt he'd earned it.

That went down so smoothly he drank another.

He went way back with these guys. They were part of the gang that Seth had introduced him to at boarding school. They'd stayed tight ever since. Seth was the first of them to get married. He knew there was a kind of melancholy to them hanging out getting hammered while Seth was off having sex with his new wife.

This was the way of the future. One by one, they'd all get married or move across the country for new jobs or whatever. Their carefree youth was slowly coming to an end.

It was how life was meant to work. But, while they were all still here, minus one, they partied.

Of course they didn't exclude women from the party, and between the dancing and the drinking and the laughing, it was late when Jackson figured he'd better call it a night. Cynthia tried to slip him her room key but, even though she was an attractive woman and he was a single man, he couldn't work up the enthusiasm. He claimed he'd drunk too much and took her number. Which he knew he'd never call.

The band had packed up, and the tired-looking bartender gave them the fish eye. He knew they were going to be a sad and sorry bunch come morning.

He got to his feet.

"Okay, I gotta go to bed."

To his surprise, all the guys rose at the same time.

"Jackson—" Willy threw drunken arms around him "—you're too drunk to drive. I'll walk you home."

He opened his mouth to tell Willy none of them would be driving and realized there was no point even trying to reason with Willy.

"Have to be quiet," Rip warned them, staggering along. "People sleeping."

"Right."

They piled into the elevator. He pushed the number three. Nobody pushed another button. Seemed they were all on the same floor.

The whole mob of them stumbled down the corridor. He rooted around in his pocket. Pulled out a valet parking ticket. Nope. Other pocket.

There it was. His room key card.

Willy grabbed the card out of his hand. "Allow me," he said, as if he were the bellhop.

"You angling for a tip?"

They all snickered as if he was Chris Rock. Willy stopped at a door and made an exaggerated gesture. "Your room, sir."

"No, my room's down there." At least he thought it was.

Willy shook his head. "Good thing we walked you home."

He stood back and waited. Willy was more wasted than he'd thought. When the key didn't work, he'd... well, his room was around here somewhere. Down the hall. He'd find it.

But, to his surprise, when the key slid home, the green light glowed.

Willy opened the door, put the key in his hand and patted him on the back. "Night, Jack."

"Yeah, night."

Right before the door snicked shut, he heard a gale of laughter. He shook his head, wondering what they'd found to laugh about and hoping they all made it back to their rooms okay.

He stripped rapidly and stumbled into the bathroom. Peed, brushed his teeth. Damn, he'd bought the spearmint toothpaste by mistake again.

He drank a huge glass of water, knowing his morning self would thank him. Then he flipped off the bathroom light and walked back into the bedroom where he fell, naked, into the king-size bed.

As he closed his eyes, he smelled something light and floral and sexy. Someone had worn that fragrance tonight. He couldn't think who, but his body stirred in memory.

He edged closer and found himself touching warm, female skin.

What?

Apart from Cynthia, one more woman had tried to slip him her room card, but he was sure he hadn't taken it.

Had he?

Oh, she smelled good.

He eased closer; the curving line of her shoulder captivated him. The curtains were open, as were the French doors, and moonlight cast the palest glow on her skin. He couldn't resist: he put his lips to the curve where her shoulder met her throat. A pulse beat there, slow and steady.

And then she made a sound like a purr and turned to him.

He wished he could remember her name. Damn.

He might be drunk—okay, he was drunk—but he wasn't going to have sex with someone he didn't even know.

He raised his head to look at her more carefully and at the same time she opened her eyes.

His heart stopped.

Her eyes opened wide.

Holy shit.

He knew this woman's name perfectly. And most

of the time wished he didn't. What was Lauren doing in his bed?

She blinked slowly, not moving or turning on the light or calling security. In fact, she didn't say anything. He recalled that moment when their gazes had caught, when she was walking down the aisle, and he'd felt that punch of—of something he had no name for. *Recognition* was the closest he could come.

For a long moment, they simply looked at each other. He wanted to apologize, but the words wouldn't come, wanted to move, no idea which way. Backward? Forward?

She lifted a hand. If she was going to slap him, he was ready. He'd explain, except he had no idea what had happened. Then he recalled the snorts of laughter after his old school buddies had walked him home, and he thought he knew exactly how he got here.

She didn't slap him, though.

She laid a hand on his cheek, slid it to the back of his head and, to his shock, pulled him toward her.

They'd kissed already tonight. That forced kiss, close-lipped and dutiful, in front of a crowd. He still recalled the feel of her soft lips under his, the light scent that was now teasing his senses.

And then she put her mouth on his.

3

JACKSON EXPERIENCED THE slam of lust, sharp and fierce, as she kissed him. Not some dry-mouthed kiss your great aunt Mildred would give you, like the one they'd shared earlier, but a deep, wet, hungry soul kiss.

He pulled her against him, feeling her soft, warm skin, the silky slide of a nightgown that was definitely in the way.

When she moved her mouth like this, he wasn't reminded of firing squads or poison ivy. He thought of hot skin sliding on hot skin, of what her nipples would taste like on his tongue, the sounds she would make when he brought her to climax.

He ran his hands lightly up over the silky gown to stroke her breasts through the fabric and felt her nipples respond, hardening beneath his palms.

Her body began to grow restless, but something about this place, the romantic location, the soft hush of the ocean coming from the open French doors, the moonlight, the wedding, made him want this to be special for her.

Their first time to be special.

Those clever artist's hands of hers began to move over his body, learning him, exciting him. When her hand closed around his cock, his hips jerked helplessly against her hand. He wanted so much more; he wanted her wet heat surrounding him and he was too excited for much handling.

As though she'd read his mind, she moved on, stroking his chest. Then she pressed herself against him as though their entire bodies were kissing.

As they rubbed and teased, she rolled right on top of him. She'd taken her hair out of its updo and it spilled over her shoulder in sexy loose curls.

He reached for her, but she kept rolling until she was off the bed.

What the hell?

Stunned, he watched her dash into the bathroom, heard rustling and then she returned carrying—oh, yes—condoms. He liked a woman who traveled prepared.

She tossed a trio of square packs on the bedside table beside him and then, still standing, the moonlight glinting on her skin, she put her hands to the hem of her short, silk gown and slowly raised it.

He watched, not daring to blink in case he missed something, his eyes taking in every superb inch as she revealed herself.

Long, elegant legs, rounded hips with that glorious triangle beckoning, then the long, lean abdomen of a runner, and the small, perfect breasts.

She pulled the gown over her head and let it float to the ground.

Naked, she walked to the bed to join him.

LAUREN HAD NO IDEA what she was doing, but ever since she'd woken to find Jackson mysteriously in her bed, she'd followed her instincts.

For all she knew, she was dreaming, and this was nothing but a wet dream.

But what a wet dream.

When she kept his mouth busy doing other things besides insulting her, he was good company. Especially naked. And as she looked at that mouth, she knew she was going to keep it very busy for the next few hours.

She slid back into bed, settled herself against him once more and put all thoughts of tomorrow out of her mind.

This was a sex fantasy, she reminded herself.

Nothing but a wet dream. And dreams were always gone in the morning.

As he moved against her, she loved the feel of his hair-roughened skin against her smoother flesh, loved the muscles—and who cared how he'd come by them, really.

When he slipped a hand between her thighs and found that perfect spot, she forgot to think at all.

Sensation. That was all she had. The quiet lap of waves outside mingled with their soft sighs as their excitement increased.

The moonlight cast the night in the colors of a dream.

The tiniest taste of scotch when she kissed him, and the taste and smell of hot, horny male when she moved her mouth down to his chest.

He played at her wetness, taking her relentlessly up. Slipping a finger inside her to stroke deep. She felt herself growing slicker, felt her hips dance in time with his knowing fingers.

The first climax took her so sweetly it was on her almost before she knew it, so she felt tossed as surely as one of those waves out there lapping the beach.

She kissed him: part gratitude, part demand.

She wanted more, so much more, and based on the rock-hard cock pushing against her thigh, she wasn't alone.

He fumbled for a condom from the night table and, with a lot more haste than finesse, sheathed himself.

When he rolled over her, she opened for him, finding, to her surprise, that she was trembling. Almost a year had passed since she'd last been intimate with a man. She'd been so busy working a second job to support her stained-glass business that she hadn't missed the time commitments of a relationship, or the sex.

Or had she?

He kissed her deeply as his body entered hers. There was a moment, when they were fully connected and his hips rested against hers, that she felt as though she couldn't breathe, that she'd fallen off a cliff without noticing it was there.

Then he kissed her once more and the strange feeling fled. He began to move, slowly at first, and then faster. When they moved together she felt stunned that their bodies had a perfect ease that their daily selves had no idea of.

She felt a kind of magic happening. His face was shadowed where he gazed down at her and she wanted to see him.

She nudged him, and they rolled together until she was on top of him, her knees anchoring her to the bed. She felt him deep inside her. As she began to move, finding the perfect angle, she felt the beginning tremors of another climax. She gripped his hands, stared into that rugged, way too gorgeous face, blue eyes that could suck a foolish woman into their depths, and rode him until her head fell back as she cried out. Even on the echo of her own cries, she heard his.

When she floated back to earth, she slumped down on top of him and he put an arm around her and stroked her back.

Hours later, her well-loved body finally fell into a deep and dreamless sleep.

Lauren wasn't sure what woke her. Her eyes felt heavy, her body completely relaxed. When she opened her eyes it took her a split second to recognize where she was and another split second for memory to flood her.

She turned and discovered what had woken her. Jackson was dressing. A glance at the bedside clock told her it was 6:00 a.m.

In the dawn light he seemed like a shadow, this man who had shared her bed and brought her so much pleasure. They'd gone through all three condoms and each time she'd thought nothing could ever feel as good. And then the next time it had been even better.

She realized that, from the time she'd opened her eyes long after midnight to find him naked beside her, until now, they hadn't exchanged one word.

As though feeling her gaze on him, he looked over at her, his Irish blue eyes questioning.

"What happened last night...?" he began in a husky voice that petered out as though he had no idea how to finish the sentence.

"Nothing happened last night," she said. And as the words came out of her mouth she understood that was exactly the way they needed to play this.

Somehow he'd ended up in her room and she re-called the expression on his face when he'd realized he was in her bed. He'd looked as shocked as she'd felt. She strongly suspected their night together had been orchestrated by the frat boys.

The best way to spoil their juvenile fun was to let them think their schoolboy antics had failed.

Nothing about last night had been a prank, or a joke.

It had been a sexual fantasy come true. If the man who'd rocked her world answered to anything other than Jackson Monaghan, she could imagine hoping this was the beginning of something.

But the man *was* Jackson Monaghan.

"Nothing. Happened." She repeated the words, knowing he understood exactly what she was saying.

To her relief, he nodded, and after opening the door carefully and glancing up and down the hallway, he sent her a wave, and was gone.

4

LAUREN SHOWERED, DID her hair and makeup with more care than usual and then dressed in the outfit she'd brought with her, knowing that she'd be seeing most of the wedding party and quite a few of the guests at breakfast.

There was no formal meal, but since checkout was at eleven, she imagined most of the guests would wander in and out before then.

She walked into the restaurant where the hotel served breakfast. She'd agreed to meet Amy's parents here for breakfast and she had a feeling that Amy and Seth would make an appearance, too. Then they'd be heading off the island and driving to LA for their evening flight to Italy, where they were spending their honeymoon.

Amy's parents were giving her a lift back to the mainland, where she'd left her car.

She quelled the cowardly impulse to hide in her room until ten fifty-five and then dash down to drop her key at the front desk and claim her ride with Amy's folks. But, she told her reflection in the mirror as she swiped a confident berry shade on her lips, that might give Jackson the idea that he'd rocked her world or something and that she was too shy to face him this morning.

That thought was enough to get her out the door with her head held high.

When she got to the restaurant it was all very unexciting. No gales of laughter or crude jokes from the frat boys greeted her. Not one of them had made it down yet. She suspected hangovers to be the cause and was only too happy to be spared.

A swift glance told her that Jackson wasn't here, either, so she was able to relax and join Amy's parents, who welcomed her with big smiles and a hug from June, Amy's mom, who was very much a second mother to Lauren.

Looking at June was like looking into the future and seeing how Amy would look in a quarter of a century. June was still an attractive woman who dressed well and never let a week go by without a trip to the hairdresser. Amy struggled with her weight, and with June you got the feeling that she'd given up the fight years ago.

"Thank you, Lauren, for doing such a fabulous job yesterday. You were the perfect maid of honor. You know we've always thought of you as a second daughter."

June got a little misty-eyed, which of course made Lauren get misty, too. "I feel like part of your family, too. It was a lovely wedding."

"It was. I was just saying to Ted that I can't wait to see the photographs. I think we got some good ones yesterday."

They settled at the table for eight, which Ted had grabbed, hoping Amy and Seth would join them as well as Seth's parents.

"Did you sleep well, dear?" June asked as she poured coffee for Lauren from the big carafe on the table. They'd known each other so long she didn't have to ask.

The more appropriate question would've been, "Did you sleep at all?" But because she tried never to lie if she could help it, she answered with a truth. "I never spent a better night."

"That's good. The beds are so comfortable that I'm going to find out where they get them and think about ordering one for home. Ted usually wakes up with a sore back, but you didn't this morning, did you, darling?"

"No. Only sore feet from dancing so much last night."

"Try it in high heels," his wife murmured.

Their waitress came by for their breakfast order, but they decided to wait a few minutes to see if anyone else would show.

"And when you see your daughter, for God's sake don't ask her how she slept," Ted said to his wife.

"But I always ask—" Then her expression changed as she realized what he was referring to. "Yes, of course not. Their wedding night." She leaned across the table to Lauren. "Sometimes I can be tactless. I never mean to be, I simply say things without thinking them through. Ted gets embarrassed by me."

"She's known you for twenty years, June. I think she's noticed."

Lauren hadn't had enough sleep to be able to come up with the right response so she sipped her coffee and hoped Amy and Seth would show up soon.

Seth's parents arrived next. Natalie and Lance. Lance, like Seth, had been a college football star in his day. He'd worked at the family real estate firm, married a pretty girl from a good family and lived a country-club lifestyle. His son was well on the road to being exactly like him.

As the two sets of parents settled at the same table, she was conscious of how careful they were around each other. Clearly, they were all trying to get along.

"The wedding was absolutely perfect, June," Natalie gushed. "I can't remember a lovelier wedding. Exactly what we would have chosen if we had a daughter."

"And Amy's a great girl," Lance added. "Great girl."

"We couldn't be happier to welcome Seth to our family," June countered. Ted made a noncommittal sound that could have meant anything. Lauren was fairly certain that he was having trouble accepting that his little girl was all grown up now and had another man in her life.

While they drank coffee, the first frat boy staggered in. Behind him was the rest of the sorry crew.

Ted eyed them in distaste. "I'll be lucky if last night's bar tab doesn't ruin me."

"Oh, Ted," his wife said. "We've got plenty of money. And they certainly look well punished this morning. Good morning, boys," she called out.

"Morning," they all mumbled. Those who weren't up to mumbling nodded.

"Breakfast?" the cheerful hostess asked them.

"Coffee," Willy groaned.

She saw Willy and a couple of other guys glance at her curiously, then at the empty seats on either side of her. She said, "Good morning," and went back to her coffee.

As they were being seated at a table close by, Jackson strode in.

His timing couldn't be worse, for now they had an audience of people to witness them seeing each other for the first time since he'd left her room at six this morning.

His hair was wet and he was wearing sweats. He'd clearly been working out in the hotel pool or the gym or somewhere. Compared to the frat boys, Jackson was a poster boy for clean living. If she hadn't known absolutely, positively that he hadn't slept all night, she never would have believed it from looking at him. His blue eyes were clear and bright, and he carried himself with energy.

He greeted everyone generally. His gaze skimmed over her and she willed every cell in her body to stay calm and not to even think about making her blush.

She did not want to feel fluttery. Jackson was an entitled twit who was completely full of himself and did everything he could to make himself a chick magnet. She'd always prided herself on being immune to him.

Now, thanks to a stupid prank, she'd ended up naked in bed with the man and nature had taken its course. Maybe if they hadn't been at a luxurious hotel and alcohol had not been consumed and they hadn't found themselves all but naked in the same bed, nature would have left them well enough alone.

However, what had happened, had happened. She had no regrets. If anything, last night had reminded her that she was a woman who really liked sex and that she'd gone way too long without it.

Why, it had been rather nice of Jackson to come along and give her such a thoroughly satisfying wake-up call to her own needs. Now she could go on with her life and meet someone who would not only give her great sex but also wouldn't make her want to gag with his annoying personality.

She knew that, hungover as they were, the frat boys were still watching her and Jackson closely.

It gave her immense satisfaction to see that Jackson looked and acted exactly the same as he always did. And, to her relief, she could tell that she neither blushed nor squirmed.

Good thing they couldn't see inside her, where everything was aflutter. So long as the frat boys didn't check her pulse, they'd never know how successful their little trick had been.

"How are the heads this morning, boys?" Jackson asked, giving Rip a good-natured slug on the arm.

"The shooters may have been a mistake," a chubby guy named Chad admitted.

Seth walked in at that moment, followed by a faintly blushing Amy. The distraction was exactly what Lauren needed. Now all eyes were on the newlyweds.

"Morning, everybody," Seth said, looking heavy eyed and pleased with himself.

Jackson was preparing to sit with the frat boys, but Seth stopped him. "Come on, bro, keep the wedding party together one last time."

Lauren felt his hesitation. He wanted to sit at the same table with her as much as she wanted him there. Which was to say, she'd rather go out front and eat sand right off the beach.

But with Ted and June, plus Natalie and Lance, joining in, encouraging him to sit with them, there wasn't much he could do. "Sure," he said. "Thanks."

There were seats on either side of Lauren, and one in the corner beside Ted.

He squeezed past June and Ted and took the empty seat that was as far from Lauren as he could get.

Oh, she could do better than that. With a big smile, she said, "I don't want to split up the bride and groom. I'll move so you two can sit together." And she moved in the opposite direction to Jackson, taking the seat as far away from him as the table allowed.

Amy settled herself beside Lauren, and as Seth made to join them, he glanced at his school buddies and said, "Toilet paper in the bridal suite? Really, guys?"

"At least one of our pranks worked," Rip muttered, too hungover to keep his voice down.

Her gaze went immediately to Jackson, who glanced at her at the same moment. His face never changed expression, but he sent her the ghost of a wink.

While Seth, with his excellent manners, thanked both sets of parents for the fantastic wedding, Amy leaned in to Lauren and in a very low voice said, "That was the best night of my whole life."

She looked so blissed out that Lauren couldn't help smiling. "It's not like it was your first time," she reminded her best friend.

"I know, but being married made it so much more special. Every time he touched me, I thought, 'This is my husband,' and when he kissed me and looked right into my eyes I felt like he was looking into my soul."

As happy as she was for her friend, Lauren experienced a pang of worry. Amy sounded almost too happy. She'd always been such a romantic that Lauren feared she was going to be disappointed when the real world intruded on her fantasy.

Then she mentally smacked herself. She was cynical about marriage for a lot of reasons that had nothing to do with Amy or with marriage. She should be happy that Amy was the kind of person who believed that perfect love existed. Maybe she'd even been lucky enough to find it.

So, Lauren put away her cynicism for a minute and squeezed Amy's hand. "I am really happy for you."

"I hope one day you find a man like Seth. I really do."

She smiled, but knew that a man like Seth would never do for her. He was a nice guy, in his way, but, like Amy, he'd never been tested by life. He'd grown up rich, healthy and sheltered. He didn't seem like a person who thought deep thoughts or had big dreams. He'd work in his family's business, as he'd been born and bred to do, and he and Amy would have a few kids and join the right country club. She hoped they'd continue to be as happy as they were today, or at least manage to enjoy the future that she could see rolling ahead like a movie of the week she'd already seen.

"You were such a beautiful bride," she said, because she'd rather talk about Amy's wedding than the likelihood that she would ever end up with someone like Seth.

"You were such a great maid of honor. You're the sister I never had."

"I don't know how I got so lucky," she replied.

It was true. The odds that she and Amy would have ended up best friends were insanely low. She'd only met Amy because after her parents divorced, her mom had rented a former pool house on the property next door to Amy's parents.

Since they were the same age, they'd played together all summer and in the fall, when she'd started school, Amy had already been her best friend.

Lauren's mom worked long hours as a nurse and Amy's mom, wonderful woman that she was, had opened her home and her arms to the lonely child. She'd often gone over to Amy's after school and had so many sleepovers at her friend's place that she'd started leaving extra clothes and a toothbrush over there.

Her mom had done her best, but she'd always been tired from work and bitter over the divorce. She'd been only too happy to let someone else help rear her only child.

Lauren's dad had married again soon after the divorce and she'd overheard more than one telephone argument between her parents as her mom complained that he didn't take Lauren often enough.

As her father went on to have a second family, she'd seen less and less of him. The pain had softened, but she knew herself well enough to know that she would always bear the emotional scars.

Her mother had remarried not too long ago, to a radiologist she'd met at work. Her mom finally had the big house she'd always wanted and she'd cut her work hours way back. They tried to be close, she and her mom, but deep down she knew it was an effort for both of them.

"Excited about the honeymoon?" she asked.

"I can't wait. Remember when you and I went to Venice? I always thought it was the most romantic place in the world. I picture us eating wonderful food, and seeing all the sights. And having fantastic sex every single night." She shivered. "I love being married."

Lauren had decided on eggs Benedict for breakfast, but when the waitress took their order, to her annoyance, Jackson ordered eggs Benedict. She decided to change her order to something else, then mentally chided herself. If she wanted eggs Benny, then that was what she'd order. So she did. Like Jackson, she also ordered freshly squeezed orange juice. Because she wanted it.

After breakfast, she packed up, freshened up once more and then headed down with her travel case. She dropped off her key and was waiting in the main foyer for Amy's parents when Jackson came toward her with his own overnighter. She knew the second he caught sight of her. His steps faltered and she could see him debating whether to duck off into one of the hallways or face being alone with her.

After an infinitesimal pause, he continued toward her.

She was pretty sure that, in his shoes, she'd have ducked down another hallway.

When he got close to her, she saw that he had a newspaper tucked under his arm and a take-out coffee. He stood close but not too close. Nodded.

She checked her watch. Eleven on the dot. Where the hell was everyone?

"Well, we got through it okay," he said.

"Yes. We did."

She did not want to have a conversation with this man. She wanted to be far away from his annoying presence and the hot, hot memories it evoked.

He clearly felt the same. He moved a step away and flipped open his newspaper.

Not to be outdone, she pulled out her cell phone and checked her email.

Not that there was much email on a Sunday. She had an invitation to submit a piece to a curated exhibit, which was flattering. A note from a supplier that the copper oxide she'd ordered was going to be delayed, which didn't please her at all.

Since she didn't want anyone thinking she was the kind of loser who got only two work-related emails on a summer weekend, she took her time replying to both of them. By the time she was finished, Amy and Seth had arrived with both sets of parents in tow.

Amy and Seth were driving their own car and heading to the airport. Seth's folks were driving back to their home, and she was riding with June and Ted to their house where she'd left her car.

Since they were all heading to the same ferry back to the mainland, they saved the hugs and final goodbyes.

The Ruehls' Lincoln pulled up in front and the valet attendant flipped the trunk and helped load their luggage.

"Jackson," June Ruehl said, "can we offer you a lift back to the city?"

"No, thanks, June," he said. "I'm catching a ride back with Willy."

"All right, dear. We'll see you soon."

When they were all settled in the car, Lauren in the backseat, June gazed out the window at Jackson, who was throwing his case in the back of Willy's Mustang. "That Jackson is such a lovely young man," June said. "I wish he could find a nice girl."

5

THE TROUBLE WITH being an artisan, Lauren decided as she picked up her soldering gun and prepared to turn chunks of colored glass into art, was that it gave her too much time alone with her thoughts. Sure, she could join an artisans' co-op, share a warehouse with painters and sculptors and potters, but she'd never wanted to. She created alone.

However, that meant there was no easy way to distract herself from her thoughts and her memories.

Those memories were hotter than the metal liquefying under her solder iron. She knew exactly how it felt. For the curated show, she'd decided to make a window that paid homage to the impressionists. She always liked the music in her studio to reflect what she was working on so she had Debussy playing in the background.

When she was in the midst of designing, nothing got in her way. Her mind was completely focused. But once she got to the semi-mechanical state of production, it was too easy to drift. And for some insane reason, her thoughts inevitably found their way to That Night.

How was it possible that a guy she couldn't stand could be the one to have brought her so much intense pleasure? It didn't make any sense. And, even worse, every time she thought of that night, her body grew restless and wanted more.

She was going to have to make time to get out more. Start dating.

Guys were always hitting on her in the tasting room at the winery. She always turned them down, but maybe she should start being more open. Why not?

She wished Amy were here. This was what a BFF was for. Times like this when you were stuck in your own head and something wild and crazy had happened. Who else could she talk to?

But Amy had left on her honeymoon. She'd received a short email from her telling her that Italy was fantastic and that she was having the best time ever. She'd ended her post with "ciao" and a happy face.

Which was great. But Lauren had to accept that now that Amy was married, she wasn't going to be as available for everything from girls' nights out to Saturday morning brunches and shopping expeditions.

Life as she'd always known it was changing.

She glanced at her watch and then began putting away her tools. She was on shift at two o'clock and it was almost one.

She didn't make a huge amount of money pouring wine in the tasting room, but her meager wage came with a cottage on the property. She'd also wheedled the use of one of the outbuildings as a studio for her stained-glass work. The winery was family owned and run, and since she liked the owners as well as the wine, she enjoyed her job. Besides, having to get out there and interact with people stopped her from getting so caught up in her craft that she became a weird recluse, something that Amy insisted would happen to her if she didn't work out a better balance in her life.

Whatever.

Back in her cottage, she showered, quickly put a few curls in her hair with the curling iron, slapped on some makeup and slipped into jeans and a crisp white polo shirt with the Leonato logo on the pocket. The only reason her work shirts were crisp and always gleaming was that they were sent out for cleaning and pressing.

She strode up the gravel road, enjoying the sight of all those green grapes fattening on the vines. The sun was warm and her work was going well.

If she could get rid of the constant buzz beneath the surface of her skin when she thought of That Night, she'd be having a really great day. A week had passed—when was she going to stop waking at night, hot and restless, reliving the hours of bliss? This had to stop soon.

She let herself into the back of the low, wooden building that housed the offices and the front tasting room. The Leonato family had come from Sicily and a tradition of wine growing. The same varieties of grapes did well in Napa and the business had grown.

She heard the buzz out front that suggested quite a few people had decided to tour wineries on this sunny June Saturday afternoon. She hurried through to the front and immediately got busy.

She'd been doing this job for three years now, ever since she'd finished art college. Naturally, artists didn't generally make a living wage, but she'd been lucky in finding both a job and a place to live. The Leonatos had commissioned her to create a showpiece window in this very tasting room and even carried some of her creations, so long as they were wine-related.

She'd come up with a line of stained-glass wine holders, each one unique, that sold pretty well during the holiday season.

After three years, she was adept at reading the people who came in. She could identify the tourists who could barely tell red wine from white, and the wine snobs who liked to discuss varietals and soil and the weather of each particular vintage. Some of them were big spenders, others time wasters.

Usually, they started visitors on the simpler, cheaper wines. If they showed real interest or knowledge or were obviously planning to buy something, she would move them on to taste the premium wines.

Usually, everybody had a good time. Including her.

Today was typical. When she walked in, Sharon Leonato was pouring samples for a well-dressed couple she seemed to know.

She nodded when Lauren walked in. They'd catch up when they had a break.

Lauren checked stock, opened a new bottle of the standard Shiraz, wiped down the counter. A guy in his thirties strolled in with a woman he was clearly trying to impress. Lauren offered the guests the regular spiel that went with each wine, but the man soon took over from her, giving his date more in-depth knowledge than she probably cared for. He waved away the first-tier wines and went straight for the premium. Since Lauren had a strong suspicion he was going to continue trying to impress his date by buying an expensive bottle or three, she happily obliged.

Two couples came in, well dressed and obviously enjoying each other's company. As she served them, it turned out that one of the couples was from London and, while visiting their friends in California, were planning to cook a gourmet meal. They'd come to the winery to purchase the wine for dinner. After an hour of tasting, they bought a case of wine to take with them. She rang up the sale with a pleasant feeling of accomplishment. She hadn't been pushy, but she had a way of encouraging people she knew could afford it to splurge a little. Why not? Both her livelihood and that of the Leonatos depended on it.

As they were leaving, the British woman caught sight of her wine coolers and raved about them so much—even picking one up and carrying it to the window so she could see how the sun streamed through the panes of colored glass—that her husband gave in and pulled out his credit card.

Sharon caught sight of the transaction and walked over to tell them that Lauren was the artist. Of course they raved some more and the woman even asked Lauren to autograph the little card that went with the cooler.

"Lauren created that window for us," Sharon told them, indicating the stained-glass creation. It depicted the Leonato family crest surrounded by grapes and foliage in big, bold colors. The window might not be what she'd have created without their input, but that was the thing with commissions. You had to give the customer what they wanted.

Yes, she thought as she waved them away, today had been a good day.

A minivan pulled up and out piled twelve older people. Leonato was listed on a few wine tours and they often got groups coming through.

She and Sharon exchanged a look and Lauren reached for the bread crisps they kept in bowls on the counter. The idea was to use the crisps to cleanse the palate between wines, but they'd found from experience that the tour bus groups usually feasted on them as if they hadn't been fed for days.

This group was no exception. They sampled their wine and emptied all the bread bowls while either listening to her descriptions of the various wines, or pretending to. The tour guide, Michael, added information about the region and then reminded them to make use of the restrooms as it would be more than an hour until their next stop.

The group made some modest purchases and took a few photos.

Lauren waved the last of them off and then began refilling all the bowls.

Her skin prickled suddenly and she glanced up.

Jackson had just walked through the door.

For a second, she thought this was just another one of the sexual fantasies that had plagued her over the past week. He looked so good. His dark brown hair that had felt so thick and luscious when she ran her fingers through it had the shiny look of a recent washing. He wore a beat-up leather jacket, a black T-shirt that hugged his torso the way she longed to, and jeans that molded to his strong thighs.

He walked over and sat on one of the bar stools in front of her. "Hi," he said.

"Hi." A million thoughts jumbled together in her head, ranging from *What the hell are you doing here?*

to *Do me, now*. She didn't voice any of them, though, and simply stared at him.

"I took an afternoon off," he said. "Thought I'd taste some wine."

Wine tasting. Of course. That was where they were. In a wine-tasting room. "You came to the right place," she managed. She put the bag of snacks away and was suddenly thankful that her spiel was so practiced she could describe each of the Leonato wines in her sleep.

She handed him the menu. "Welcome to Leonato," she said.

"Thank you."

She knew she should launch into her standard speech about the winery and each of the wines, but she didn't have it in her. She said, "Take a look at our wines and let me know what you'd like to try."

He didn't even open the handsome leather folder with the Leonato coat of arms emblazoned in gold on the front of it. He gazed at her face. "What do you like?"

She felt hot and cold flashes dance over her skin. What did she like? Who knew better than he did? In one night he'd brought her more pleasure than she'd experienced with anyone before.

She felt like telling him in exact detail exactly what she liked in case he might have forgotten in the past seven days. She felt like begging him to take her somewhere and do every one of those things to her until she could get some relief from the wanting.

Instead, she pulled herself together and said, "My favorite wine is our cabernet sauvignon from 2011. It won some awards. Normally, we don't sample that one, but we opened a bottle earlier, if you'd like to try it."

"I'd like to try it," he said.

She poured him a more generous glass than usual. Watched him sip and savor. He nodded. Then his eyes crinkled around the corners. "I don't know a lot about wine, but it tastes good to me."

An older couple came in at that moment and, when she would have excused herself to greet them, Sharon, who'd been at the other end of the wooden bar polishing glasses, rushed forward. "I've got it," she said.

Sharon was always trying to get her interested in any single men who came into the tasting room, so Lauren wasn't surprised.

Under the hum of conversation, she wondered if Jackson would say something to her, maybe tell her why he was here. But, no. He acted as though he really had just stumbled into this winery out of all the wineries in Napa. "Have you toured many wineries today?" she asked him.

"No. Just this one."

"I can give you a map. There are lots of amazing wines in this area." She rolled her eyes at her own inanity. Jackson was as cool and distant as if they were complete strangers, and she was tripping all over her nervous tongue. "Obviously. This is Napa," she added inanely.

"Okay," he said. He took the map but didn't seem in a big hurry to open it.

"Have you heard from Seth?" she finally asked, thinking maybe he was here because something was going on with Amy and Seth.

His eyes crinkled again. "He's on his honeymoon. I got a one-liner from him saying Italy was awesome."

He took another sip of the dark red wine. "You? Heard from Amy?"

"Just a quick email. Sounds like they're having fun."

There was another pause. He finished the wine in his glass. Put the empty goblet down.

"Would you like to try something else?"

"No, thanks. I'll take a bottle of that, though."

"Sure."

She grabbed him a bottle, wrapped it and took the credit card he offered. Once she'd rung up the purchase, she gave him his receipt.

"Thanks," he said. "See you around."

"Yes. See you around."

She watched him walk out, wanting to run after him and drag him back to her cottage. The way the man filled out a pair of jeans was almost too good to be true.

She had no idea why he'd come here. All she knew was that his little visit wasn't helping her squelch the demon of lust that had overtaken her body.

Shaking her head, she moved to clear away his empty glass. And then she froze. Those hot and cold shivers danced over her skin once more.

Beside the empty glass was a key folder, the kind they gave out in hotels.

She glanced up, but he was gone.

Her heart began to thud. She didn't think he'd remembered to take his wallet, his credit card and his receipt and somehow accidentally left his key card folder on the counter.

She didn't think it was an accident at all.

She picked up the paper folder, which had the name of the hotel on it. She knew it. A nice inn not far from the winery. She opened the folder. Inside, in handwriting that she recognized as Jackson's, was a room number: 505. Underneath it he'd written, "Tonight!" And underlined the word.

6

As Jackson strode to his car, got in, carefully stashed the bottle of wine and started the engine, he wondered if he'd completely lost his mind. What kind of a jack-ass gave a woman a key to his room? No invitation to dinner, no personal chitchat of any kind, just a key and what amounted to a dare. A challenge.

The truth was he'd no sooner thought of asking her to dinner than he'd rejected the idea, knowing she'd spurn the offer in an instant. They didn't want to sit across a table from each other over dinner and talk or get to know each other.

They already knew each other and didn't like what they knew. She was cold, superior and sarcastic, and he certainly wasn't going to put a dinner invitation out there for her to scorn.

But he had a problem.

He couldn't get their night together out of his head. He thought about her when he was at work, when he was trying to sleep at night; when he was in the shower, when he was driving.

The surprise he'd felt when she'd turned out to be

not a cold fish in bed but a warm—no, hot—exciting woman still hadn't worn off. He thought that was probably why he'd been obsessed with memories of that night. Nothing about their night together had been expected, from the moment he'd seen her emerge in her bridesmaid dress looking softer and prettier than he'd ever imagined to the moment he'd walked out of her room the next morning, his body sated and his mind blown. The entire affair had ended only a few hours after it had begun.

He hadn't nearly finished with Lauren. He wanted one more night, under more normal circumstances than a booze-fueled, unexpected rendezvous in a honeymoon hotel complete with moonlight and ocean breezes.

One more night.

He'd known that she worked part-time at the winery and, assuming she'd probably be working on a busy Saturday afternoon, he had taken a little road trip and discovered that he'd been right. She was working.

When she'd spotted him, he'd had the pleasure of watching her blush slightly, looking for a moment as though she was really happy to see him. So far, so good. Then her usual cool mask had descended.

He'd left her that key and the note. The rest was up to her.

Okay, so he'd chosen an inn that was on the classy side, also a popular honeymoon destination—mostly so she'd show up. Maybe he wasn't planning to take her to dinner, but he wasn't going to bed her in a roadside motel, either.

He liked to show a little class where women were concerned.

But would she show up? That was the question that gnawed at him as he showered and shaved with care. He didn't know what time she got off work, so he settled in front of the TV and tried to concentrate on the news, a movie, a football game. He left the game on in the end, but he wasn't really following the play. He kept wondering, would she come to him?

Or had he just made the biggest mistake of his life? He could imagine her now, texting her girlfriends, telling the fine wine samplers of Napa about his foolish move between sips of Shiraz, blogging about the loser who'd left her his room key. For all he knew, that was exactly what she was doing.

But the woman who had shared her bed and her body with him wouldn't do that. She might not show up in his hotel room, but she wouldn't be cruel.

Daytime Lauren, he wasn't so sure about.

LAUREN GOT THROUGH the rest of her shift somehow, with the key card and its provocative note stuffed into the back pocket of her jeans, where it burned like a warm hand resting there.

Sharon hadn't missed how seriously hot Jackson was. She fanned herself the minute he left and commiserated with Lauren that he hadn't stayed longer. "A man like that and a bottle of wine? Sounds like heaven to me."

Sounded like heaven to Lauren, too.

Would she go?

Would she do it?

There was something admittedly exciting about having a hot guy show up and slap a key card down in front of you. No, "Hey, I really missed you." No invitation to dinner or "Let's get together for a movie." Just "Let's get to it, babe. Here's the hotel room key, and isn't it your lucky night?"

When she thought of the sheer arrogance of the man, assuming that, first, she'd be free on a Saturday night and second, that she'd drop everything to fall into his bed, she was tempted to toss that key into the trash.

But then she imagined him asking her out for dinner or a movie, and the idea was impossible. What would they talk about over a long dinner? They had absolutely nothing in common, didn't even like each other. What they had was purely chemical. That was all this was.

And when she thought about that, she respected that he wasn't pretending that this *thing*, whatever it was, was any more than sex between strangers.

Okay, great sex between two people who might like each other better if they were strangers.

So she smiled, she poured, she got subtly hit on, she got not so subtly hit on, she took credit cards, she wrapped and boxed bottles, and at the end of her shift she was no closer to a decision than when Jackson had sauntered out of there three hours ago.

Was she going to go to him or not?

She walked home and flipped on the lights. Her tiny cottage felt ridiculously silent.

She shucked her jeans and the polo shirt that was basically her uniform. Got into the shower. She shaved, because really, who didn't love smooth skin? And when she'd dried herself off, she slathered on a heavenly body lotion that Amy had bought her for her birthday. It was the kind of expensive luxury she'd never have bought for herself.

She brushed out her hair so it swung around her

shoulders, and slipped into the nicest set of lingerie she owned, which she'd bought for Amy's wedding.

Amy. If only she were back. She wanted to pick up the phone and call Amy so badly it hurt.

But things had changed. Amy wasn't going to be available at all hours anymore. She was married. And in Italy.

"Why are you putting on makeup?" she demanded of her reflection. And continued sliding smoky shadow over her eyelids, adding two coats of mascara and then slicking a tinted gloss over her lips.

But she knew why she was applying makeup with care and wearing sinfully rich body lotion and wearing barely there lingerie. Because her body was humming with excitement.

And why Jackson Monaghan should be the one to set her humming like a tuning fork was beyond her comprehension.

She threw on a simple cotton dress for two reasons. One, the color looked great on her and two, the dress was easy to take off.

But she didn't rush out of the door and into her car.

She hovered.

She watered the plants.

She paced.

And, while she hovered and watered and paced, she thought about what she was contemplating doing.

The first time she could blame on chemistry and the reaction of two naked people finding themselves in the same bed in a fancy hotel, after consuming large quantities of alcohol.

The second time? That involved planning.

The key card was in her hand. It was on the table

and the handwritten word, *Tonight!*, taunted her. Like a promise, a dare and a tease, all in one.

She couldn't think about tonight and not be reminded of that other night when something as unexpected as it was magical had happened between them.

What if the second time ruined it? Maybe they should leave well enough alone.

In fact, there were a lot more reasons not to go to Jackson and only one reason to turn up. Lust. Pure, horny lust.

Lust that was pricking at her with sharp fingernails, urging her to go to him.

When her cell phone rang, she thought it was Jackson checking on her, but of course he didn't have her number. She glanced at the call display and saw it was Amy. Damn, that girl might be married, but she was still the best friend Lauren had ever had and they were still close enough that she'd picked up on her friend's dilemma and was calling.

"Amy!" she cried as she answered. "I was just thinking about you."

"I know I said I wouldn't call from my honeymoon, but I had to," Amy said, her voice sounding choked.

All thoughts of Jackson and sex flew from her mind. "Are you okay?"

"No-o-o-o." A sob answered her. "Me and Seth had our first fight."

Visions of a terrible accident, the theft of all their belongings, a mugging, a death in one of their families fled thankfully back to the recesses of her mind where worry lived, and a tiny flicker of amusement took their place. "Your first fight? You've been together, what?

Three years? And you've never had a fight?" Of course they hadn't or she would have heard about it.

"No." Amy dragged in another choked breath. "We've always been so happy. I thought our love was perfect."

"Honey." She sat down on her couch. "No love is perfect." Then, realizing Amy probably hadn't called to hear her talk, she said, "What happened?"

The story that poured out wasn't very dramatic. It wasn't even all that interesting. The only thing that made it either of those things was that Amy seemed so shocked to discover that she and Seth weren't going to be in perfect harmony for every second of the rest of their lives together.

They'd been getting ready to go out and he'd snapped at her that she was always late.

It was true, as Lauren knew better than anyone. Amy would always be nearly ready and then decide to change her outfit, or decide she was hungry, or that she just needed one second to send an email she'd forgotten she needed to send right away. Lauren was used to Amy's habits and she'd have thought Seth was, too.

After he'd snapped at her, Amy, stung, had snapped back that she'd be on time if she wasn't so tired of constantly cleaning up after him.

"Honestly, Lauren, he's a slob."

"Didn't you know that?"

"Not really. I think he always cleaned up before I came over and now he doesn't bother. I told him that I'm not his mother."

Ouch. "Then what happened?"

"He went out. And he slammed the door. I don't know where he is or when he's coming back. I don't know what to do," she wailed.

"Maybe you two need to talk. Marriage is an adjustment. It's going to take some time to get used to each other being around all the time."

"I guess. I used to go home to my place so I always had a break from him. But now, he's in my space all the time. Do you have any idea how much noise he makes when he brushes his teeth? Seriously, it's like a construction crew doing roadwork in there. And he makes noises when he sleeps."

"You mean he snores?"

"It's more like heavy breathing. It's driving me nuts."

So, she let Amy unload, knowing she wouldn't be asking her best friend's advice on whether she was going to go to Jackson or not.

She was on her own for that decision.

SHE WASN'T COMING.

Jackson popped a grape off the fruit and cheese plate he'd foolishly ordered from room service in case she arrived hungry.

It was nine o'clock and the leaden feeling in his gut was disappointment.

When his cell phone rang, he jumped for it, and then realized it couldn't be Lauren calling because Lauren didn't have his cell number.

Wouldn't be getting it any time soon, either.

When he saw that it was Seth, he answered immediately. "Hey," he said. "How's it going down there?"

"Don't ever get married," his old friend warned him.

"Seth?" He could hear the noise of a bar in the background, loud conversations and louder music. "Where are you?"

"I don't know, a bar somewhere in Venice."

"What happened?"

"We had a fight."

He had to hold back a laugh. "Dude, everybody fights."

"Not us. We never fight. She used to be so sweet." He slurped a drink. "And hot. So hot."

"You've been married a week. I seriously doubt Amy has lost her looks."

"I'm telling you, the minute you get married, everything changes. I used to get to her place and she'd be all dressed up for me. Now I have to watch her getting dressed. And seriously, she wants input. Like, do you think it's cold enough for a jacket? How the hell do I know the external temperature if I haven't been outside, either? Does she think she married a meteorologist? And then, do I like these shoes? Or these shoes? And don't think you can get away with randomly pointing, because you can't. Then she accuses you of not listening."

"You've been with Amy a long time. How did you not know any of this?"

"Because it was different," he bellowed. "Even the sex."

"Don't tell me about the sex." He seriously did not want to hear details. But short of hanging up on his oldest friend, there wasn't any way to shut the guy up.

"You know why there aren't any jokes about married sex?"

He was pretty sure there were plenty, but he kept his mouth shut and listened.

"Because it's already a joke."

Even though he'd never gone into any explicit detail, Seth had always led him to believe that Amy was great in the sack. What was going on? "I thought you two had awesome sex."

"It's not as exciting anymore. I wake up, she's there, beside me in bed. I go to bed, she's there beside me in bed. Where's the fun in that? I look ahead and I realize she's always going to be beside me in bed for the next forty years, day in and day out."

"Kind of what you signed up for," he offered.

"We had a fight."

"Yeah. You said. Good. You should fight. It's healthy."

"She said I'm a pig."

Having roomed with the guy Jackson knew it to be true. "You are a pig."

"See, when you say it, it's okay. When she said it, she made it sound like I treat her like a servant. She even brought my mother into it."

"Oh, that's low."

"I don't know what to do. I'm sitting here on my honeymoon alone in a bar and it isn't even noon."

"Go back. Tell her you're sorry. And remember, it's normal to fight."

"On your honeymoon?"

He had no idea. "Just go talk to her. You love Amy and she loves you. You'll work it out."

"I guess." He blew out a breath. "So, what are you doing on a Saturday night? Getting ready to bang some hot chick, I bet."

Well, he was certainly ready, but it looked as if the hot chick in question wasn't coming. "I wish," he said.

As he hung up, he decided, since he was in this fine suite, that he might as well enjoy it. He uncorked the wine he'd bought from Lauren, poured himself a glass and shucked his clothes, slipping into the sumptuous robe provided by the hotel.

It wasn't cold, but he switched on the gas fireplace anyway, and settled in an armchair with a book.

He'd barely read two pages when the *thunk/whirr* of the key card sliding home and the lock opening announced he had a visitor.

She didn't bother knocking.

When she stepped into the room, he didn't speak, simply stared at her. She was so gorgeous, with her hair loose and a soft cotton dress molding to her exquisite body.

"I didn't think you were coming," he said.

"I didn't think so, either."

His heart was pounding and simply the sight of her standing there had him growing hard. "What made you change your mind?"

She walked to him with her long stride. Then she took the book out of his hand and placed it on the table. She hoisted a leg over and settled on his lap. Taking his face in her hands, she kissed him, long and deep. He knew the second she touched him that their crazy night hadn't been a dream.

She pulled away, her eyes already growing heavy lidded.

"This," she said and lowered her mouth to his once more.

7

THE FIRST TIME had been random, spontaneous. The second was different because it was deliberate. He'd driven a long way, gone to a lot of trouble to get a room and drop her a key with a taunting note.

She'd shown up.

And now that she was here, she couldn't imagine depriving herself of that mouth of his, those hands that seemed as though they knew instinctively where to touch, what she liked.

Beneath the hotel robe she could feel him hard and ready for her and the knowledge made her wet and ready for him. His fingertip traced the V of her dress from her collarbone to where the two sides of fabric joined over her breasts. As his fingertip traced the line, she felt shivers run over her skin, igniting stronger reactions in her nipples and her core.

He followed the line of the dress to where the wrap belted in front. "What happens if I pull on this tie?" he asked, his voice smoky with desire.

"Why don't you pull it and see what happens?"

He did, so slowly that it seemed as though the messy

bow she'd made when she put the dress on earlier was struggling to stay whole. The loops took endless time, growing smaller while she and Jackson both watched.

When the tie finally gave, she felt them both give a sigh of relief. He still didn't rip the dress off her; he took his time, easing the fabric away, revealing her slowly.

Even though he'd already seen her naked, she felt as though he was savoring the experience all over again.

When he'd pushed the dress off her arms, and let it fall slowly around them, he pulled her forward so he could put his mouth on her, right through the lacy cups of her bra. She sucked in a breath as the sensations shot, wild and crazy, through her.

"You smell so good," he said, "And you taste even better."

He smelled good, too, and he tasted good, so good. When she reached forward to kiss and taste him some more, he slipped his hands behind her and unhooked her bra. He slid the silky straps slowly down her arms, and she felt him enjoying the view as he bared her. The room was dim but for the flickering of the gas fire, which added atmosphere and pulses of warm light over her skin.

She wanted to see him, too, to feel herself skin to skin so she wiggled out of his arms only long enough to strip off her panties, feeling his hungry gaze on her as she did so.

Then she slipped onto his lap once more. And she ran her fingertip down the V of his robe. Slowly, torturously. She felt the warmth of his skin, the roughness of hair, the bump of a nipple. When she got to the tie, she asked, "What happens if I pull this?"

He was having as much fun as she was. His grin was intimate and daring. "Why don't you pull it and we'll find out?"

She did. Maybe not as slowly as he'd done hers. She didn't have as much patience. But she took her time. She felt him holding himself in check, knew he was impatient to be inside her and that he was letting her set the pace.

When she finally had the tie undone, she opened the sides of the robe slowly, as though she were unwrapping a particularly decadent chocolate.

It wasn't that she'd forgotten what he looked like, it was more that she doubted her own memory. She assumed that she'd fantasized the absolute perfection of his body.

But she hadn't. His skin was tanned and she couldn't imagine how many hours he must spend in the gym to get those abs, the pecs, the arms.

He wasn't wearing any underwear, which made her very happy.

She touched, she stroked, she tasted and nibbled, and a few times she bit lightly.

He did his own touching, stroking, tasting and nibbling until they were both breathing heavily and she knew that it would be painful to tease each other any longer. She grabbed one of the condoms she'd brought from her bag, which she'd dropped beside the chair. She took her time sheathing him, enjoying wrapping her hands around that strong, gorgeous cock.

Then she maneuvered herself so her legs were spread wide over him where he sat on the chair, positioned him at the entrance to her body and sank slowly down.

He filled her, stretched her, anchored her, and then

they began to move together. Blue, Irish eyes stared up at her, intense and focused as though she was the only thing in the world he cared about. The connection between them when their gazes met was almost more intimate than their joined bodies. Maybe he was an ass by day, but at night he was like something out of a fairy tale. The evil gremlin who became a prince in darkness, but reverted to his unpleasant alter ego when daylight returned.

He must have caught her grin. "Something about having sex with me amuses you?" He moved in time to his words so she could barely hold on to sanity.

"I was thinking you're like one of those fairy tales where you're an evil troll by day but by night you turn into a magnificent prince."

She thrust down hard as she said it, rocking against his pelvis. She didn't think anyone had ever reached so deeply inside her before.

He thrust up against her as if he could push in a little deeper, as though he could never get deep enough. "Seems to me," he said, "that in those fairy tales it's usually the woman who's an ugly hag by day, but in the moonlight changes to a gorgeous princess."

He reared up out of the chair, so fast she had to wrap her legs around his hips to hang on. He held her, walked with her, until she was pushed against the wall, and where she'd had control of the pace, now it was all his.

She was so open, so stretched, and it was like nothing she'd ever known.

With each thrust he was hitting both her clit and her G spot, and she was starting to see stars.

"You saying I'm an ugly hag by day?" she managed, sounding dreamy to her own ears.

"I'm saying you're gorgeous in the moonlight," he said, thrusting deep. She felt the tremors of a climax begin deep inside her. "And the firelight." He thrust again, taking her over the top. She cried out, kissing him, squirming against him, crazy with wanting even as the wanting was over. She felt him lose control at the same moment so they cried out together, their mouths still joined.

The moment stretched to eternity and back again and then a glorious sense of Yes filled her.

He walked them both to the bed, still connected, and slowly lowered her down. They lay together, recovering their breath, and then she put her mouth on his chest, where his heart thumped beneath his skin.

She tasted salt and heat and felt that she'd reached a new level of high she'd never reached before. Knowing they'd need to rest up a little for round two, she settled against him.

"Do you want a glass of wine?" he asked.

"Sure."

He rose, naked and gorgeous, and strode to the table where the open wine sat. The firelight glistened on his skin and she drank in the sight of his muscular back, the tight, round butt, the long legs that were strong enough to hold both of them up while they made love against the wall.

He poured two glasses and returned to the bed, handing her one and putting his own down. Then he returned for the cheese and fruit plate and settled in bed with it.

He passed her the tray and she helped herself to a slice of brie and quarter of pear. Munched. Sipped her wine.

"How can you have great sex with someone you don't even like?" she asked.

He shrugged as though searching for answers, too. "Everybody says Steve Jobs was a jerk, but I still like my iPhone."

He leaned over and kissed her shoulder, a brush of his lips that had her wanting all over again. "And for the record I thought it was great, too."

"Do you think, if we actually liked each other, that the sex would get dull?"

She thought he might not answer. He took his time selecting a grape and said, "That's never going to happen, so we won't have to find out."

During that long, incredible night she discovered one thing for certain. The magic between them hadn't been a onetime thing.

If anything, the sex was better the second night.

But, like all nights, it had to come to an end.

As dawn broke, Lauren eased out of bed. Jackson had fallen asleep only a few minutes ago and she knew that if she didn't leave now, she'd fall asleep, too. And one thing all those fairy tales had in common was that getting caught in the daylight was bad news for the prince or princess under the crazy-ass spell.

So she crept over to her clothes and swiftly dressed, then grabbed her bag.

As she crept to the door, she paused, turning to take one last look at her sleeping lover. The man she despised by day and was beginning to crave by night.

She put two fingers to her lips and sent him a silent kiss. Then she let herself carefully out, wondering when she'd see him again.

8

AMY CALLED LAUREN almost the second she was back from Italy, full of giggles and wanting to meet for lunch to tell her all about the honeymoon.

Lauren had never been so happy to hear from her best friend. She wanted to talk to Amy, to tell her about the madness of this crazy affair with Jackson, to see if she could make sense of it by talking it through and maybe get Amy's advice.

Amy had a flexible work schedule. She worked part-time for an interior designer who pretty much let her set her own hours. And, since Lauren didn't have to work at the winery today, a long lunch was definitely on the menu.

They chose a little place near the wharf with a great view of the bay and good food. When she spotted Amy, she grinned. Clearly, her friend had found time to go shopping in Rome. She wore a summer cotton dress that screamed designer and shoes that made Lauren swoon.

They hugged. "You look fabulous," she told Amy. She did, too. Lightly tanned and happy.

Amy groaned. "I don't. I ate so much. I couldn't help it—the food was so amazing. But between the bread and the pasta and the wine, I must have gained fifty pounds." She patted her stomach. "I am going on a diet." She picked up the menu and sighed. "Next week."

"How many diets will this make?"

Amy lowered her menu. "Easy for you to say. You are so naturally thin. I should hate you."

Lauren returned her fake glare. "You are so rich. I should hate you for those shoes alone."

"You know what they say. You can never be too thin or too rich. Between us we are the perfect woman."

Then she passed Lauren a bag with Italian writing on the front of it. "What's this?"

"Something from Italy that I thought you might like. I would have brought home one of those gorgeous, brooding Italian men, but he wouldn't fit in my suitcase."

Lauren opened the bag and gasped with pleasure. Inside were a lacy black bra and a pair of matching panties. "Italian lingerie? Are you kidding me?"

"I know your wardrobe and you really needed some new lingerie."

Oh, she had no idea.

"So? How was the honeymoon?"

"Italy is so beautiful. I loved every second of it. The food, the art, the history. Even the weather was perfect." She rattled on about Rome (kind of dirty and crowded, as she'd remembered, but the shopping was fantastic and so was the Colosseum) and Florence (as pretty as the postcards made it look) and Venice (she'd forgotten that it smells, but she got used to it, and the gondola ride by moonlight was so romantic).

"So everything worked out okay, after you and Seth had your first fight?" Lauren asked.

Amy's lips tightened. She'd known the woman too many years not to be able to read her every expression. This one said she didn't want to talk about it. Probably regretted her hysterical honeymoon phone call. "Oh, sure. It was just a blip. We're so lucky to have found each other. I'm the happiest woman in the world."

"I'm glad," Lauren said.

Somehow, with Amy proclaiming that married life was perfect, she didn't feel comfortable sharing something as intimate and confusing as her sex-only relationship with Jackson. Even as she ate her organic greens and goat cheese salad, she realized that telling Amy would no longer mean telling only Amy. No doubt she'd share what she'd learned with her new husband. And since Seth was Jackson's best friend, well, the last thing she wanted was to be a topic of conversation among the newlyweds. And, for all she knew, Seth wouldn't be able to resist telling the frat boys.

Sadly, she decided to keep her secret to herself and stay confused rather than confiding in Amy and making a big deal out of what was purely sex.

Simple, uncomplicated sex.

It wasn't as if she and Jackson were the first two people to indulge in a sex-only relationship. They were friends with benefits. Except that it was more like enemies with benefits, which made the entire thing a little strange.

But sitting there, listening to Amy talk about her plans for decorating her home and how she and Seth had signed up for a gourmet cooking class so they could host better dinner parties, she began to feel that her oldest friend was slipping away. Of course she was. It was only natural.

"And the first person we're having over for dinner is you. You have to see your window now that we've had it installed. It looks so good. Makes me happy whenever I look at it."

"You had it installed already?"

"Yeah! One of the benefits of working for an interior designer is knowing so many tradespeople. I love it so much. It's my favorite wedding gift. Truly. I wanted it in my house right away so I always feel like my best friend's with me."

She'd really put her heart and soul into that piece and was so happy that Amy loved the small window. She'd created an abstract design with the blues of the ocean that Seth and Amy both loved, using the circle, the symbol of eternity, as her main motif. She'd done the window in an art deco style to complement the era in which the townhouse had been built and embedded a subtly entwined *A* and *S* to personalize it.

"So? Are you free Saturday night? For dinner?"

"This Saturday? Um, sure, I guess." Truthfully, she wasn't thrilled at the idea of dinner for three when it included Seth.

But it turned out Amy had something quite different in mind. "Seth wants Jackson to come for dinner, too."

Her heart made an uncomfortable bumping motion inside her chest. "Jackson's coming, too?" She was sure she sounded less than thrilled.

"Yes. Well, what can I do? He is Seth's best friend. But not to worry. We both didn't want to stick you with each other when you don't get along, so we decided to invite two other people."

The way she said the words "two other people" made Lauren suspicious. She hadn't said "couple," which made it sound as though she'd invited two other singles along with Lauren and Jackson. Amy fiddled with her knife and fork instead of looking straight at Lauren.

"Who are these other two people?" Lauren asked.

"Don't get weird, okay? It's not a setup. Not exactly. Daniel is in banking. He just got moved here from London and doesn't know many people. His family and Seth's family go way back. So Seth thought it would be nice to invite him. He's single and very eligible. We stopped in London on our way back from Italy and I met him. I tell you, if I wasn't totally in love with Seth, I'd go for him. He's hot. And that sexy British accent—mmm."

Of course, Amy couldn't even begin to know what an awkward situation she was setting up. "You know I hate blind dates."

"It's not a blind date. It's six people having dinner together."

"Who's the sixth?"

"Someone we thought Jackson might like. You remember Sylvia? Who I used to work with?"

"The architect?" Her voice rose slightly. Sylvia Yang wasn't only an architect, she was one of those people with so many accomplishments she was completely intimidating. She'd been a championship rower in university, spoke her parents' Cantonese plus a few other languages, was on the fast track with the architecture firm she'd joined, and she was stunning to look at. "I can't believe she's single."

"I know. She was dating a hotshot lawyer for a while,

but they were both so busy they hardly ever saw each other. I think she's getting to an age where she's thinking of settling down."

Well, good luck with that if she thought Jackson was ready to settle down.

"We're going to cook an authentic Tuscan meal. We brought home the most incredible olive oil and, well, trust me, it's going to be great."

Yeah, right. But how could she turn down her best friend?

JACKSON AND SETH played squash at Seth's club after work. It was a routine they'd established when they'd first ended up working in the same area, Seth for his family's real estate firm and Jackson for the start-up.

After the game and shower, they met up in the lounge for a beer. Seth rubbed his wedding ring as though he was still getting used to it.

"How's married life?" Jackson asked him. They hadn't had time to talk since the semi-drunk honeymoon phone call.

"It's great. Amy's an angel."

"Good. So you got over your first fight?"

Seth laughed, a boisterous *ha ha ha*, as though he'd forgotten he'd ever called. "Yeah. It was the stress of the wedding, that's why we had the fight. I looked it up on the internet. Do you have any idea how high on the stress scale getting married is?" He rubbed his wedding ring again, polishing it the way Aladdin polished his lamp. "I mean it's right up there with divorce and death. I had no idea."

Jackson wasn't sure that comparing marriage to divorce and death when you hadn't even been married a month was a great sign. However, Seth obviously didn't want to talk about it, which was fine with him.

"So, we bought all this crazy good stuff in Italy and we're cooking Saturday night. Can you come?"

"For dinner? With newlyweds?" He felt nauseous at the idea of being stuck with Seth and Amy while they cooed at each other.

"Not only us. Amy wants to invite Lauren, obviously."

He had a momentary glimpse, a fleeting memory of Lauren walking toward him, swinging her leg over and settling herself on his lap. "Lauren's coming?" His voice came out slightly hoarse and he had to clear his throat.

"Don't worry. We won't stick you with her all night. We're adding a couple of other people to the mix."

"Define *other people.*"

Seth got a kind of cagey look about him. "Look, it was Amy's idea and I have to do what the little woman says." He had actually called her "the little woman." Jackson was so stunned it took him a while to hear the next words that came out of Seth's mouth. He had to concentrate, rewind and catch up. By which time it seemed as if Seth and Amy were so pleased with each other and married life that they were going into the matchmaking business.

"Wait," he said. "Let me get this straight. You're inviting two other single people to your dinner? One for me and one for Lauren?"

Seth looked embarrassed, as he should. Since when did guys engage in matchmaking? Might as well get out the pink wool and start knitting toilet roll covers with yellow woolen roses on top. "It's not a big deal.

We didn't want you and Lauren taking chunks out of each other at the dinner table, that's all."

When he thought about taking chunks out of Lauren he thought of the way her skin tasted when he nibbled on it and the sounds she made when he grazed his teeth lightly over her nipple. Being set up with another woman while she was in the room was going to be interesting. Not that he and Lauren would ever go on a date or anything. Obviously, this sex thing was a temporary madness that would burn itself out. Still, he was curious. "Does Lauren know about this?"

"Yeah. I guess. Amy told her when they had lunch."

"And she was okay with it?"

"I think so."

And why should that make him feel weird? It was stupid to think she was saving herself for him, but somehow he'd assumed that neither of them were sleeping with other people. What would he do if he found out she was having sex with another guy? Or guys?

He thought about it and knew the answer. First, she wouldn't have sex with him if there were other options, any more than he'd welcome her into his bed if he had another woman in his life. They didn't like each other. They were obviously sleeping with each other because that was the best option available.

He thought that if someone else came along, maybe the champion rower architect, he'd be ready to move on.

Probably.

No doubt Lauren felt the same way.

"Who have you lined up for Lauren?" He pretty much knew all the guys Seth knew and couldn't imagine any of them appealing to Lauren, who seemed to him to be impossible to please outside the bedroom.

"Guy named Daniel Putnam. You don't know him. His dad's a friend of my dad. He got transferred to San Francisco from London. He's a stock analyst for one of the big banks." Seth seemed to scan his memory for anything else he could add. "Plays polo."

"Polo?" Guy sounded like a total dud. Lauren would hate him.

"Well, he's British," Seth said as though that explained it.

Jackson dreaded the dinner from that moment on. He'd have bailed, pretended he had other plans, but he couldn't. If Lauren was going to go through with a dinner that included newlyweds, a man she hated but was sleeping with, and two other singles, then he was going to go through with it, too.

One thing he knew for certain, it would be an interesting evening.

9

WHAT DID YOU WEAR to a dinner party both your blind date and your secret lover would be attending? Lauren asked herself the question as she flipped through her wardrobe one more time.

It wasn't an extensive wardrobe. Mostly, her clothes ran to jeans, the kinds of shirts that she could burn, stain with metallic oxides or generally ruin, and a few nice outfits for going out. Most of which she'd already worn for Amy's wedding-related events. She'd never known how much socializing was involved in getting married.

She called Amy, as she always did when she had a clothing dilemma. "What should I wear for dinner Saturday?"

Amy knew her wardrobe as well as Lauren did, and it didn't take her long to mentally scan it. There was a short pause before she said, "What about the cotton wrap dress? It shows off your figure and the color's great on you."

It was the same dress Jackson had unwrapped just a few nights ago, which made the dress seem like a very bad idea. If she wore it, she knew he'd get the wrong idea. "I don't think it's good enough for British aristocracy," she said.

Amy laughed. "Every man who plays polo in England is not aristocracy. Why don't you borrow something? I've got more clothes than I can ever wear." Amy wasn't boasting. They'd known each other so long, she was simply being honest. She loved shopping and money had never been an issue for her, which meant she owned way too many clothes, and too much stuff in general.

"Please. I'm not a charity case."

"We always borrow each other's clothes," Amy said, sounding mystified. It was true, although, admittedly, it was usually Lauren who borrowed Amy's much nicer clothes, but the possibility that Jackson might recognize her wearing one of Amy's outfits made her skin crawl with hot embarrassment. Not that he'd probably even recognize any of Amy's clothes, but she'd know she was wearing borrowed feathers. Likely Seth would, too, and he might tell Jackson.

"I think I need to go shopping," she said. "I'm a big girl. I should get some more going-out clothes."

"Ooh, excellent. I haven't had good retail therapy since—" Lauren paused. "Okay, since my honeymoon two weeks ago. But this is different."

"And I need your help."

"Cool."

So they went shopping. Lauren spent most of her money investing in her business, but for once she listened to Amy and decided to splurge on an outfit. She went with a local designer Amy knew about whose prices reflected the fact that she hadn't been discovered yet.

"Yes," Amy announced when she tried on a summer-blue dress that hugged her waist and flowed over her hips.

Naturally, a new dress needed shoes. And then Amy had to try on a few dresses and shoes of her own. "Because I got so fat in Italy, I can't fit into anything." She always had an excuse for spending money.

"How about coffee?" Lauren asked as they strolled past a coffee shop.

"How about lipstick?" Amy countered, pointing across the street. "You should update your cosmetics every season, you know."

When they headed out of Sephora, Amy turned to her, her eyes sparkling. They were both wearing their new lipstick colors and carrying bags replete with their updated cosmetics. "Brit boy won't be able to keep his eyes off you. Trust me."

"Amy," she said, feeling as if she needed to tell her best friend about her and Jackson. But when she tried to form the words to explain, nothing came to her.

Amy stared at her for a second and then said, "It's only dinner. We'll have fun."

"And Jackson's definitely coming still?" She fumbled as one of her bags threatened to slip. "I mean, I don't want to feel like a third wheel with Ms. Champion Rower and The Brit."

"Yes, he's definitely coming."

Happily burdened with shopping bags, and not so happily burdened with her secret, she headed home, where Lauren was struck with guilt over the chunk of change she'd put on her credit card and promptly went to work on a new line of wine holders for the winery. Stock was low and the holders provided a nice stream of extra income for her.

Besides, keeping her hands busy and her mind focused helped her ignore the jumpy feeling she had about Saturday.

BEFORE SHE KNEW IT, Lauren was standing in front of Amy and Seth's door holding a bottle of the cabernet that she'd last drunk while lying naked in bed with Jackson.

Stop it! she ordered herself, and she rang the bell.

Amy opened the door wearing a stunning skirt, the blouse she'd bought on their shopping trip and yet a different pair of Italian shoes that smote Lauren with envy.

"You look fantastic," Amy said, pulling her in for a hug.

"You, too."

Amy dropped her voice to a near whisper. "Wait till you see him. He's even cuter than I remembered." Amy fanned herself. "His accent is so much sexier in America than it was in the UK, where everyone sounds like him."

Chatter and soft music drifted from the living room, and after thanking her for the wine, Amy led her into the house.

"Lauren," Seth said, rising from his seat and coming forward for a hug. "Great to see you."

"Hi, Seth. Good to see you, too."

"Come on in. I think you know everyone but Daniel."

She walked in and felt Jackson's presence as strongly as if they were alone, naked and touching. How did he do that to her? Her gaze went unerringly to his.

He looked so good. He'd made a real effort with his appearance, she noted, for Sylvia Yang no doubt. His eyes were ridiculously blue in the navy shirt he wore, no doubt, for that very reason. His pants were hipster narrow and he wore leather shoes that looked brand-new.

Out to impress, was he?

With effort, she dragged her gaze away from Jackson to the man who had risen and was advancing on her with his hand outstretched. *Wow*, was her first thought. Amy hadn't exaggerated. He really was exceptionally good-looking. Daniel had hair so brown it was almost black, and sleepy dark eyes that were oddly out of sync with his prep-school smile. He wore a blazer with an open-necked shirt, gray trousers and hip-looking boots. He could've been a model in an ad for British cologne.

As he took her hand he pulled her closer and kissed her cheek. *Smooth*, she thought. *Practiced*.

"Pleasure to meet you, Lauren," he said. Amy was right. The accent was definitely sexy.

"Nice to meet you, too."

"Come sit beside me and tell me all about America," Daniel said, drawing her over to the seat beside his.

"America's a pretty big place," she said, settling beside him and accepting the glass of prosecco Seth handed her. They were going Italian all the way tonight.

She sipped the bubbly wine.

"Then tell me how to make myself agreeable to American women," he said, a teasing light in his eye that suggested he didn't think he was going to have any trouble doing just that.

"I doubt we're very different from British women. What works there will probably work here."

"But there are cultural differences, surely."

"If you want to make yourself agreeable to American women, you should talk to Jackson over there. He certainly thinks he knows how to please women."

"I don't hear any complaints," Jackson said, giving her a look that suggested she was plenty pleased with him.

"American women are very polite," she said. "They don't want to hurt a man's feelings."

"And some American women are impossible to please," he argued back.

"Don't mind these two," Amy said brightly. "They always insult each other like this."

It was crazy. Insane even, but exchanging insults with Jackson was making her hot. She glanced at him and got the momentary impression that it was having the same effect on him.

She turned back to Daniel. "Amy said you got transferred here with your job. What exactly is it you do?" Not that she was all that interested, but if she kept talking to Daniel, she could ignore Jackson.

"I'm basically a stock analyst. I research companies, stay on top of trends and make recommendations for our private banking team."

"Wow. That sounds—" *boring* "—um, interesting."

"It wouldn't be everybody's cup of tea but I enjoy the work. Lot of stress, of course. Billions of dollars are at stake, but so far I've managed to do all right."

Obviously more than all right since his transfer was also a promotion, according to Amy.

An interruption occurred when the door chimed again and Sylvia Yang entered the room. Lauren's first thought was that she was glad she'd splurged on a new outfit and cosmetics. Everything about Sylvia screamed success. Her red dress was obviously designer, and Lauren remembered admiring that same summer handbag in the window of the Furla store. After greetings had been exchanged and she'd been introduced to Daniel and Jackson, Sylvia settled beside Jackson. For tonight, at least, it was clear who was paired with whom.

Once they'd resettled, and Seth had poured Sylvia a drink, Lauren heard Jackson ask her about her work. A safe topic, and Sylvia seemed happy to talk.

"And what about you, Lauren? What is it that you do?" Daniel asked, bringing her attention back to him.

"I make stained glass."

"You mean, like, church windows?"

Amy jumped in. "Lauren makes the most incredible contemporary art out of colored glass. Come and see what she made Seth and me for our wedding gift."

"Oh, no, really," Lauren said feeling like a kid whose mother forces them to play the piano for company.

But Amy was already up and Daniel rose, too. What else could the poor guy do when Amy was so insistent? "She designed it specially for us. There was already a window in the landing, but it was so boring. Wait until you see what she created."

Daniel followed Amy, and to her horror, Sylvia rose, too. "I'd love to see your work." And then Jackson tagged along, as well. Only Seth stayed behind. "I'll get started on the antipasto," he said, but Amy was so busy singing her praises that Lauren doubted she heard.

When the tour group reached the landing there was still enough light to reflect the blues and soft grays of the piece. Amy said, "You should see it in the morning sun. It's like waking up to sun and waves. We love it."

"That's absolutely incredible," Daniel said, slipping an arm around her waist.

Sylvia moved closer to the window and studied it carefully. She didn't praise or gush; she inspected. "How do you find your windows hold up?" she asked. She didn't sound like she was being bitchy, more like she genuinely wanted to know.

"Structurally, a well-made window should last hundreds of years, maybe thousands. Look at Chartres or Notre Dame. I've been doing windows for about five years now and haven't had any problems. You definitely need to know what you're doing, though."

Sylvia nodded. She took a step back and studied the window from other angles. Was she going to point out a flaw? Everyone watched her in silence. Then she turned to Lauren. "Do you take commissions?"

Lauren was so stunned to find that Sylvia wasn't about to offer criticism that she didn't say anything for a second.

"Of course she does," Amy said, launching into sales mode again. "You should see the window she made for Leonato winery. It's a real showpiece."

"Do you have a card?" Sylvia asked.

"Yes." She cast a grateful look to Amy, who was the one who had insisted she needed to get business cards and brochures made up to promote her work.

"I've got some of her brochures," Amy said. "I'll give you one. And you have to check out her website. Lauren repairs old windows, too. She's really, really good."

"Oh, stop," Lauren protested. "It's a craft anyone can learn."

"But you turn it into art," her loyal friend insisted.

Jackson hadn't said a word the whole time and they were all so bunched up together in the landing that they had to take turns stepping forward. As the group started to move away, he took a step toward the window. Studied it intensely. She braced herself, waiting for him to make a snide comment, but he didn't say anything.

Amy was telling Sylvia about the wine coolers now. Daniel walked with them. Only she and Jackson were left in the landing. In the gray-blue light that shone through the window, he looked pensive, more serious than she'd ever seen him.

At last he turned.

"Well?" she challenged. "Aren't you going to tell me I do nothing but make useless kitsch?"

"No." He paused as though he wasn't going to say more, then changed his mind. "You create something real and beautiful and lasting. What do I do? Create internet technology that's invisible and expendable. Your windows will be around for decades, maybe centuries. In five years, technology will be someplace completely different and the hours and months and years I've put into any given project will be meaningless. You should be proud of what you do."

Oddly, she felt more complimented than when Amy had gushed about her. "Thanks," she said. She turned and they headed back down the short hallway together. "It's not as lucrative as what you all do, but it works for me."

When they got back to the living area, Amy was handing out her brochures to both Sylvia and Daniel. "This is starting to feel like the home show," she said, shooting Amy a glance that meant, *Stop.*

Sylvia laughed. A soft, well-trained laugh suitable for all occasions. "I'm glad you brought that up. Can I see the rest of the house?"

"Oh, my gosh, of course. I'll give you the grand tour." Amy loved showing people around her new house, and who could blame her?

Daniel tagged along, but Lauren had already seen the house and knew it well, so she headed toward the kitchen, thinking she might give Seth a hand.

Jackson had obviously had the tour also, for he followed her.

"Can I help, Seth?" she asked, peeking into the kitchen. Seth was unwrapping charcuterie from the market. He turned the packaging upside down and dumped the meat on a huge antipasto plate so it landed in a meat-colored brick. The poor man really needed help. The slices needed to be arranged, coordinated with the roasted peppers and slices of eggplant she could see on a tray on top of the stove. There were various tubs from the market waiting to be opened and added to the artful arrangement Amy had no doubt envisioned.

"No, thanks, I got it," he said. "Too many cooks and all that." He reached for another package.

What could she do but go and sit down? She took a sip of her prosecco.

While everyone else was otherwise occupied, she and Jackson were left alone together in the living room.

She sat awkwardly on the couch, nursing her wine. He appeared equally awkward, taking a seat on a chair that was as far away from where she was sitting as the small room would allow.

When she felt his gaze on her she picked up a magazine from the coffee table. She knew it was rude, but she didn't care.

In her peripheral vision she saw Jackson pull out his smartphone.

A minute later, when she had no idea whether she was reading *Time* or *Cosmo*, her cell phone chirped, signaling a text message. Anything was preferable to the pained silence in the room, so she dug into her bag for her phone.

She didn't recognize the number. The text read, This is weird.

She glanced up and saw that Jackson had his phone in his hand. Not looking at her but with a tiny, almost smile on his too-sexy mouth.

She texted back rapidly. How did you get this number?

His answer was immediate: Borrowed your phone when you were sleeping.

Why did he have to bring that up? The words conjured an image of the two of them tangled together in bed, so exhausted that she'd fallen asleep. Her waking to find his mouth on her nipple, pulling gently until she moaned and turned to him.

Before she knew how to respond, he texted again. My place tonight?

She glanced at him, and found him looking straight at her, those deep sleepy eyes offering her everything you could pack into one night. But his place? That was a big step up from an anonymous hotel. His place was where he lived, where his things were, where he slept every night, where he kept his books and his music. She'd find out whether he was a neatnik or a slob, what kind of food he kept in the fridge, whether he had pets or tropical fish or house plants.

Did she really want to know any of those things? The more anonymous she could keep sex with Jackson, the better off they were.

But the drumbeat of desire was already getting louder.

And yet, she wasn't interested in being available every time they ended up near each other. She didn't think she wanted to be a convenience.

She texted back. Maybe.

She thought his lips quirked when he read her response, but she stuck her nose back into her magazine so it was hard to be certain.

When her text signal sounded again, she found nothing but an address.

Which was as much of a challenge and a dare as when he'd visited her winery that day and walked out, leaving behind a key card.

He might be an egotistical twit, but the man could definitely throw out a sexy dare that was as good as foreplay.

When the tour group returned to the main room, still complimenting Amy on the beautiful home and her decorating style, Seth plopped the antipasto plate in the middle of the dining table. "Antipasto's up," he announced.

The table was laid to perfection. Lauren recognized most of the items from the wedding gift registry list. Everything sparkled with expensive newness from the crystal glasses to the plates and linens.

"Come, sit at the table," Seth said before they sat down in the living room again.

Amy glanced at the table and her face pinched. "Darling, I said I'd do the antipasto," she said, sounding teeth-grindingly brittle. "Just a moment." She whisked the large platter off the table and disappeared into the kitchen, Seth stomping after her.

"What the hell?" Seth yelled. "What's wrong with my antipasto?"

"You have to arrange everything properly. You can't just dump piles of artichoke hearts and olives and chuck huge lumps of charcuterie around. There's an art to it."

"It's food. People will eat it and mess it up again."

"Please keep your voice down," Amy whispered, but her whisper was almost as loud as his complaints. "Go and pour the wine."

"You sure you can trust that I won't screw it up?"

"Just try not to spill any on the new tablecloth." She sounded so mad her voice was vibrating.

Lauren, realizing that all the guests were struck dumb with embarrassment or too busy eavesdropping to converse, threw herself into the breach. "I would love to go back to Italy. The food there is so good."

"Oh, God, yes," Sylvia said, helping her out. "I'd go for the shoes and the clothes alone."

"For me, it's the glass. Venice changed my life."

"Is that when you decided you wanted to work with stained glass?" Sylvia asked.

"Yes. It was like I'd look at the glass and my fingers would practically itch to create something similar. I started with blown glass, but moved on to stained glass not too long after."

Seth strode out of the kitchen. His cheeks were ruddy with anger and he held two bottles of wine like clubs. He used them to wave the hovering group of guests toward the table. "Sit down. The antipasto will be out in a minute. When my wife finishes decorating it."

As Jackson brushed past Lauren to take his seat where his place card, handwritten in calligraphy, directed him, he muttered, "Never getting married."

She shot back, "Who'd have you?"

10

WHEN THE GUESTS were settled around the table, Amy brought out the much-better-arranged antipasto. "I love the way they present food in Italy. Food isn't just nourishment—it's art, as well. Seth and I were so taken by the array of colors and textures, weren't we, honey?" And Lauren knew that it was Amy's way of apologizing to Seth. She hoped he understood.

Thankfully, the food was excellent and the wine plentiful. Daniel was amusing and clearly out to be charming. Sylvia and Jackson discovered some friends in common and soon the conversation and laughter drowned out the music playing in the background, always the sign of a good dinner party.

As Seth and Amy brought out the dinner they'd cooked together with all their new gadgets, she felt not only the thrill they were getting out of playing house, but something else.

Something that worried her. They seemed to be so careful with each other. It was almost as if they weren't only playing at house, they were playing at marriage.

Only it wasn't a game.

"So, Lauren, do you live here in the city?" Daniel asked, breaking into her thoughts.

"No. I live in Napa. Wine country."

"I hear it's beautiful there. Maybe I'll come up and taste some wine at your winery one of these days."

Without her meaning it to, her gaze flew to Jackson's. How could she not remember the last time a man had driven up to Leonato especially to see her? And how could she ever forget the way it had ended, with a lot more than wine being tasted and savored.

She saw Jackson shift and cross his legs and knew that he'd had a momentary flashback, too.

"There are some fantastic wineries in Napa," she said as neutrally as she could.

"We should all go up sometime," Seth said, sounding relaxed now the meal was finished. Not having to drive anywhere, he hadn't held back on the wine at dinner. He turned to Amy. "We definitely need to fill up the new wine fridge, right, honey? And then we can all go for dinner after. Take Lauren. What do you think?"

"Sure. I'm always happy for an excuse to go to Napa," Amy agreed. She turned to Daniel. "They have such great wineries and some good restaurants. Great hotels, too, if you need to stay over."

Lauren refused to so much as glance Jackson's way since they both knew one of those hotels pretty intimately.

The evening wound down, and Lauren was surprised to find that she'd had a good time. It was nice to get away from work, to dress up and socialize. The food had been good, the company pleasant, and she was glad she'd come.

She even had a sex date for later.

Daniel claimed he still had jet lag so he was the first to break up the party. He took her aside before he left and asked for her number. She hesitated and he leaned in. "I'm all alone in a new city. Take pity on me. I need all the friends I can get."

He was so cute, and what was the harm? He was a nice guy and he didn't know anyone in town. Assuming she was the first woman he'd asked, she didn't want to ruin his initial impression of American women. She gave him her number and he punched it into his smartphone with flattering speed.

"Thanks," he said as he was leaving, "I really enjoyed meeting you." He leaned forward to kiss her cheek.

Soon after, Sylvia rose to leave. "I've got an early appointment with my personal trainer," she said. And it showed in her great body.

"I should leave, as well," Jackson said, rising. So, they said their goodbyes and left together, which meant she'd never know whether Jackson had asked for Sylvia's number and if he had whether she'd given it to him. Damn.

When they were gone, Amy wouldn't let her go right away. "You can't rush off. Have some more coffee. We want to hear what you thought of Daniel."

She settled back into her seat. "I thought he was very nice."

"And what about the dreamy British accent?"

"Dreamy," she agreed.

"He was totally into you," Seth offered.

"He said so?" She didn't want to think that the two men had somehow found time to discuss her when she'd been right there.

"No. But I could tell."

"I thought he was, too." Amy curled her legs under her. "What do you think? A possibility?"

"Maybe." It was difficult to be completely honest with Seth sitting right there listening to every word. He'd said he'd do dishes, but Amy had protested, saying she'd do them later. Lauren suspected she didn't trust Seth not to break her new dishes. She had a sneaking suspicion Seth thought that, too. He dropped heavily into one of the new chairs and she felt Amy wince.

"On a scale of one to ten?"

Seth leaned forward and stared from one woman to the other. "You two don't seriously rate men, do you?"

"No, darling. Of course not." Amy winked at him. "We rate them. But it's never serious." Then she turned back. "Well?"

She hadn't thought too much about Daniel's hotness so she struggled to pick a number now. After a moment she said, "Seven."

"Seven?" Seth spluttered. "That's all?"

"I liked his manners, and his accent, of course. He's nice looking, obviously intelligent, had a lot to say, some of it pretty witty."

"And that gets him a seven?" Seth looked stunned. "What's Prince William? A five?"

"It's a personal thing. For all his positives, I thought Daniel was maybe a bit too satisfied with himself."

"Women! Impossible to please." Then his eyes narrowed and he turned on Amy. "What was I?"

She reached over and patted his cheek. "To me, darling, you're always a ten." There was an edge of sarcasm to her words but the truth was that from the second she met him, she'd always claimed Seth was a ten. Since Lauren had always considered a ten to be perfect and that no man could ever be perfect, the highest she'd ever gone on her scale was a nine. She'd always been a little amused that Amy thought Seth was a ten. She'd have given him a five on a good day.

"She's telling the truth, Seth. From the first time she met you, Amy said you were a ten." She smiled at her friend with fondness. "Only guy who ever rated a ten on Amy's scale." Though there had been a few nines.

He stood, leaned over and planted a kiss on his wife's mouth. "Good to know."

When he sat back down, he said, "What about Jackson?"

"Jackson?"

"Yeah. On your hotness scale, how does he score?"

"Don't ask Lauren," Amy said, laughing. "She'll give him a negative number."

In fact, the number that had popped into her head was nine. If you discounted all the things she didn't like about him and stuck only to hotness, he was solidly a nine, damn it. But she laughed along with Amy. Seth seemed in the mood to press the issue. He turned to his wife. "What about you? Where would you rate Jackson on the scale?"

She made a face. "I don't know. I never really thought about it. I know he's hot and all, but he's not my type. I guess a seven or eight."

Seth was clearly pleased to have rated higher on the scale than his best friend. Luckily, neither of them pressed her for an answer.

"What about Sylvia?" Amy asked Seth. "How would you rate her hotness?"

"I wouldn't mind seeing her all hot and sweaty in a singlet, bent over the oars."

"Seth!"

"What? She's a rower."

"You're supposed to give a number, not a sex fantasy."

"Okay. I'm new to this." He sipped the last of his wine. "Well, you two are both tens, obviously, and she's an eight."

Amy seemed satisfied with that. "I totally think Sylvia's going to call you," she said to Lauren. "She really seemed interested in your work."

"The way you were pimping me out, what choice did she have but to pretend she was interested?"

"No. When we went on the tour, she asked me a lot about what other work you've done and your training and stuff. She'd be an excellent contact. Imagine all the jobs she gets. A lot of their work is renovating old houses, and you know how many of them either have old windows that need fixing or some idiot took out the old stained-glass windows in a previous reno and now the new owner wants to stay true to the original design and put them back in. That's where you come in."

"I agree. It would be great to get on with another architect." She already worked with a few and she was perfectly certain that Amy had passed on that fact to Sylvia, probably also given her any names she could remember so that Sylvia could check with them before hiring Lauren. Sylvia seemed very careful. She wouldn't hire Lauren if she wasn't sure she'd produce a good project and deliver on time.

Even though she'd taken it easy on the wine and

had been drinking nothing but water and coffee for the past couple of hours, Amy tried to convince her to stay over in the guest room. "Come on, it'll be like old times. You always used to sleep over."

She laughed. "Yeah, but we shared the same room, remember? I'm not sure Seth would be thrilled."

"Come on, stay. You don't want to drive all that way home."

"It's fine. Really. Traffic will be light this time of night and I need to get a lot of work done tomorrow."

That was true. She also had one more stop to make before she headed back to Napa. Even though she'd said maybe to Jackson, she knew she was going to his place. From the glance he'd sent her when he'd said his goodbyes earlier, he knew it, too.

She'd get up early and leave Jackson's to get home in plenty of time for a full day's work. That part she kept to herself.

Before leaving, she did excuse herself to the guest bathroom, where she swiftly brushed her teeth and her hair and refreshed her lipstick.

Then she hugged both her hosts and headed out into a soft San Francisco night.

JACKSON LIT SOME CANDLES. He knew it was cheesy and he wouldn't even own candles if a coworker hadn't pressed them on him after she got carried away at some home party where the hostess invited a bunch of women over and tried to sell them a load of crap. "I've got enough candles to light up Grace Cathedral," she'd said. "My husband will kill me if he sees how much stuff I bought."

He lit a couple of the big, chunky ones that smelled like beeswax. He'd absolutely refused to take anything with a fake scent or an unmanly color, so he'd ended up with neutral beeswax pillars. He had to admit that once he had the wick flaming and the honey smell started to rise, he kind of liked them.

He opened the doors to his balcony because that was the best part about his place, the view. And then he waited.

He was pretty sure she'd show this time. Not a hundred percent, but sure enough that he brushed his teeth, flossed and shaved. He intended to check out some seriously sensitive skin and he didn't want to leave whisker burn behind. He even changed his sheets. Not that he was a pig or anything, but he thought she'd appreciate fresh linens.

He put the music on low. And he waited.

She arrived about thirty minutes later. Even her voice on the intercom turned him on. Sexy. "Come on up," he said and he'd never meant it more.

When she knocked on the door, he opened it so fast her fist was still raised in midknock. He pulled her inside, and pushed her up against the wall even as he kicked the door shut.

His mouth was on hers so fast she couldn't have spoken if she'd planned on it.

For a second, he felt her shock and then she melted. He heard a *thunk* that he assumed was her purse hitting the floor, and then she was all over him, as crazy for him as he was for her.

"Oh, I love summer," he said, reaching down and finding her legs bare.

"Mmm," she replied, nipping his lip with her teeth.

"I love this dress, too, I've been wanting to get you out of it all night."

But now, even undressing her seemed too much to handle. Instead, he hiked her skirt above her hips, slipped her panties down in one less-than-smooth move, let her step out of them and then rose, running his hands up her most excellent legs. They were smooth, shapely, the skin soft to the touch. He was sheathed in a second, and then he took her, right there against the wall, plunging up into her wet heat. He had no moves, no finesse, only naked, greedy need.

She panted, urged him on with her hands and her hips, writhing and grinding against him. She cried out way quicker than usual and he suspected that she had been half-aroused all night just as he had been. It was as though they'd already enjoyed a couple of hours of foreplay, so they were crazed with need. Her explosions set off his and he was panting, leaning his damp forehead against hers in minutes.

"Wow," she said. "That was—"

"Over too fast."

She chuckled softly. "I was going to say, intense."

Then she looked up at him, her sassy mouth curving into a smile. "Well, I got what I came for. I'll be taking my panties and going now, thanks."

He chuckled, low and dirty. "Lady, I haven't even started with you." Then he leaned down, scooped her legs out from under her and hoisted her up into his arms, he-man style. She shrieked when he first picked her up, then giggled, burying her lips against his neck.

"I always wanted someone to do that. It's so Rhett Butler."

As the candlelight cast their silhouettes on the wall, he carried her to bed.

11

MUCH LATER, LAUREN found herself curled up against Jackson. She was panting, her body still awash with pleasure and her heart thudding. Her head was pillowed on his chest, and from the way his chest rose and fell, she guessed he was panting, too. She could hear the thump of his heart beneath her ear.

"Well, that was an interesting evening," he said. She didn't think he was talking about the sex, but about earlier.

"It was. The food was excellent."

"The food was, indeed, excellent. And the antipasto platter was decorated to perfection."

Oh, trust him to take his buddy's side of things.

"Look, Amy is particular about design. And about entertaining. I don't know what he was thinking dumping lumps of stuff on the plate with no thought at all."

"He was probably hungry. Guys do stuff like that. Well, mostly we eat out of the package when there's no one around to tell us not to."

Was he kidding or serious? With Jackson, she sometimes couldn't tell. "Whatever. I think they were happy enough by the end." But she couldn't rid herself of the niggling doubt in her mind.

Jackson, however, seemed interested in something else. "So, he asked you out."

He could only have been referring to Daniel, and, since everyone had witnessed it, there was no point in denying it. "He asked for my number. He's new in town. Doesn't know many people." Why was she making excuses? She shut up.

"Oh, he'll call. And he'll ask you out. You going?" He didn't sound jealous or possessive, simply curious.

"I don't know." Her hand was tracing idle patterns on his naked belly. "It feels weird."

"Hey, it's not like we're a couple or anything. Go for it."

"What about you? You sure rushed out the door when Sylvia left. Did you ask her out?"

"No." But there was something abrupt about his answer. She thought lying on a man's chest right after sex and asking questions was as good as a polygraph.

"Did you ask for her number?"

"No." Again with the abrupt negative.

She thought about Sylvia, how direct she was, the way she'd asked Lauren in-depth questions about her work before even hinting that she liked it or might want to hire her. A woman like that wouldn't waste a lot of time waiting for a man to make the first move. "Did she ask for your number?"

He hesitated for a split second. "Yes. She's interested in what we're doing with our start-up."

"And your Irish blue eyes had nothing to do with her wanting your phone number."

He shrugged, which she took to mean that he knew

as well as she did that the architect's interest was not purely professional.

"How can we date other people if we're doing—this?" she asked.

"Well, we're not dating. It's not like anybody's betraying anybody."

But she knew what betrayal would look like and it was very clear. She raised her head so she could look right into his eyes. "Okay. But I have one stipulation. If you even think about having sex with that woman, or any woman, you warn me first so we can break this off."

He nodded. "Same with you."

She had no intention of sleeping with Daniel, but she agreed anyway.

They managed a few hours of sleep. She'd intended to wake at dawn and leave quietly, as seemed to be their pattern in the very short time they'd been having secret sex, but to her surprise, Jackson was already up when she opened her eyes. It was five-thirty and the bed was empty. She rolled out of bed, yawning. Dressed swiftly in her discarded clothes and, as she eased out of the bedroom, found Jackson looking disgustingly healthy in running shorts and a gray athletic T-shirt. "You want coffee?"

Of course she did. Desperately, but this was way too domestic, so she said, "I'll grab some on my way home."

"Okay."

She felt bleary and not at her best. She was fully aware that her hair was a mess and she was wearing the walk-of-shame clothing she'd worn last night. "What are you doing up so early?"

"I like to run in the morning. Get it out of the way."

"Even on the weekend?"

He shrugged. "I'm an early riser."

"Right. Okay. I've held you up, I'm sorry."

"It's fine."

He hesitated, and then crossed to a desk set up in the corner of his living room. He opened a drawer and drew out a set of keys. "Here," he said. "You might as well take these. You can let yourself in and out when you need to."

She glanced at the keys in her hand and then back at him. "We've never had a date and you're giving me the keys to your place?"

The five o'clock shadow darkening his cheeks was stupidly sexy. His sleep-heavy gaze rested on her. "You want to go on a date?"

"God, no."

"Okay, then. This is more convenient. If you're in town, say, and want to drop in before I get home from work."

"So I can cook you dinner?"

He took a step closer. "So you can get naked."

They barely spoke and he was giving her a key to his place?

A million jumbling thoughts all collided in her head. A key to a man's place felt so intimate.

Shouldn't they talk about this?

She should toss the keys back at him. Really, she should. If she'd had coffee and could think, that would probably be what she'd do. What was the man thinking?

But, she found herself sliding them into her purse instead.

Which didn't mean she'd use them, obviously.

WHEN HER CELL PHONE rang Monday with a number she didn't recognize, it wasn't Daniel calling as she'd expected. It was Sylvia Yang.

The architect's voice had the pleasant, crisp tone of a woman calling from her office. She didn't waste a lot of time on pleasantries before saying, "I'd like to meet for lunch one day this week. There's something I want to talk to you about."

The keys to Jackson's place practically burned a hole through her leather bag. Had Sylvia picked up on some vibe between her and Jackson that no one else had noticed? What would she say if the woman confronted her, demanding to know about her relationship with Jackson? Would she lie? "Um, lunch. Wow."

"I've got tomorrow free. How's tomorrow for you?"

She had to go into town anyway, to pick up supplies, so she supposed she might as well get it over with. She agreed to meet and Sylvia suggested a restaurant close to her work. "Sounds good."

The second the call ended, Lauren hit speed dial for Amy, but as the phone rang, she wondered what she was going to say to her best friend. She realized she didn't want her knowing about Jackson. But before she could hang up, Amy answered.

"Hey, you. What's up?"

Since she'd already called and thanked Amy for the dinner and they'd rehashed the entire evening, including Seth's bumbling attempts to help, how hot Daniel was, and did she think Jackson and Sylvia had hit it off, she didn't know what to say.

"It's so amazing that you would call," Amy said. "We're like identical twins, except for the part where we have different parents and don't look a bit alike, obviously. But we totally have that spooky thing where I'm thinking of you and you call me."

Phew. "It's because we've been best friends for so long. What's up?"

"Seth and I decided to throw a housewarming party. I wanted to make sure you're free before we set the date."

"When were you thinking?"

She mentioned a Saturday. "We thought we'd open the doors so part of it's on the patio, you know, indoor-outdoor. Kind of like our wedding was."

There was no way she could refuse to attend her best friend's housewarming even if she'd wanted to. so she made a note in her electronic organizer. "Yep. I'll keep it free."

"Fantastic. Well, I'd better go and get back to work."

"Yes. Me, too." And she was left to ponder Sylvia's strange lunch invite with no BFF to talk it over with.

Which sucked.

LAUREN DECIDED SHE wasn't going to dress up for lunch with Sylvia—it might look as if she had something to hide. Instead, she settled on wearing what she wore most days: jeans, though these were her best pair. The figure-flattering ones with no burn holes in them, and a pretty top. She put on sandals, grabbed her supply list and her bag and headed into town.

The restaurant wasn't difficult to find, even if parking was, and soon she was sitting across from Sylvia, who seemed, if possible, even more stunning, accomplished and intimidating than she had at Amy's dinner party.

She wished suddenly that she'd taken the time to get

a fresh pedicure before slipping on her sandals and that her sunglasses popped into a real glasses case with a designer logo on them the way Sylvia's did. Instead, she dropped hers right into her bag. She'd lost whatever case they'd come in, if there'd even been one.

"I'm so glad you could make it," Sylvia said as they were led to a table for two.

When their waitress came around, they both ordered iced tea and Sylvia didn't even look at her menu. "I always order the seafood salad. It's very good."

Not wanting to spend an extra minute in Sylvia's company—and, damn it, why hadn't she taken the keys to Jackson's apartment out of her bag?—she said, "That sounds good to me, too."

Before their waitress had moved away, Sylvia gave her their food order and they handed back their unopened menus.

"That was a really nice evening at Amy and Seth's," Sylvia said.

"Yes, yes, it was." She reminded herself that she wasn't doing anything wrong by having a friends-with-benefits relationship with a man Sylvia might be interested in, so she wasn't going to get all flustered and say something stupid. She took a sip of her iced tea.

Sylvia leaned in closer, an intent look crossing her face. "Look, I don't have time to waste so I'll get right to the point."

No, please, don't, Lauren felt like saying. *Waste some time, do a slow waltz around the point. Really, I'm in no hurry.*

"I thought your window was amazing."

"My window?"

"The one you made for Seth and Amy. Your stained-glass window. Their wedding gift."

"Oh, right. Of course. The window. Yes."

"I've taken a good look at your website, and I even drove up to your winery to look at the window you made there."

"Wow." Good thing she hadn't been working that day.

"Plus, I've talked to a couple of architects you've worked with in the past. Everyone speaks very highly of your work and I've really liked what I've seen."

"Thanks."

"Here's the situation. I've got a client who's renovating a mission-style home. He wants to keep the windows and some of them are in pretty poor shape, and after I saw your work I thought it would be stunning if we could commission some new windows that would complement what's there but still provide a contemporary vibe. Pretty much exactly what you did for Seth and Amy's place."

She was nodding, amazed that she'd been stupid enough not to connect Sylvia's interest in her windows with today's lunch. What was the matter with her? Of course Sylvia wouldn't be threatened by her. And there was certainly nothing to be threatened by.

She pulled her business hat on fast. "You've said that you don't have time to waste. What's the time frame?"

Sylvia smiled at her, approving. "You are correct in assuming the timing's tight."

They paused as their salads arrived and were placed in front of them, and then Sylvia continued, squeezing lemon over her salad while she talked. "We're behind schedule for several reasons, but the client's very anxious to get moved in as soon as possible. The windows would need to be installed in a month."

"How many windows are we talking?"

"Two need repair. I'd like you to assess the rest and give us your opinion. We think they're fine, but better to be certain. Eight brand-new exterior windows. A couple of interior doors."

"Dimensions?"

"You haven't run screaming down the street. Does that mean the deadline is doable?"

"I think I could do it, but I'd need to see the specs."

She stabbed a lump of crab and a chunk of lettuce. "Excellent. If you've got time after lunch, I can take you back to the office, where I can show you all the drawings and the specs. Then I'll get one of our interns to run you out to the site." She sent Lauren an apologetic look. "I'd take you myself, but I'm slammed to the wall on this project."

"Sure. That's fine."

"The faster you can get a proposal to me, the faster I can get it approved and we can start."

And just like that, one of the juiciest commissions of her career fell into her lap. It wasn't just any old house. It was a glorious old Craftsman built in the 1920s that included some of the finest deco windows she'd ever seen. No wonder Sylvia had been picky.

She was juiced with ideas and excited at the prospect. As she drove away after touring the house, she called Amy to tell her the good news. "I have to prepare a proposal. I hate this part."

"Hey, that's great! I'm so glad I bugged you about getting a decent website."

"You did. And the brochures were your idea, too."

"Now, I know you and I know Sylvia. If she needs to turn that around in four weeks, she's expecting to pay you extra for you putting everything else aside."

"I don't really have a lot of other—"

"I don't care, and neither does Sylvia. We all know you'll lose sleep and work yourself till you burn out if you have to in order to meet this deadline. Add a fifteen percent premium to your proposal."

"Really?"

"Absolutely. You're both an artist and a craftsman, and they don't grow on trees. If they did, she'd have found one by now. Look, don't waste time going to your place to work on the proposal. Come here. I do these all the time for my job. I'll help you. I'll make it look pretty and I'll make sure you don't sell yourself too cheap."

"That would be amazing. Thanks. But are you sure I won't be in the way?" Amy was married now and she had to keep reminding herself of that.

"No, not at all. I think Seth's going out tonight."

"Okay, I'm on my way."

When she got to Amy and Seth's, she was greeted warmly by both of them, and then Amy took her into her office. With three bedrooms, each of them had their own home office for now.

They got started right away. Amy was right. She was a lot better at this stuff than Lauren.

Amy was writing an intro while Lauren worked out pricing, when Seth yelled from downstairs, "Bye, see you later."

"Bye," they chorused.

She glanced at Amy, but her friend didn't seem bothered by his casual farewell. Lauren remembered how they used to kiss goodbye if one of them was going into another room. But this? Leaving without giving his new bride a kiss goodbye? Maybe for other couples it would be normal; for Seth and Amy, it seemed cold.

"He's playing squash with Jackson," Amy said, as though she'd read Lauren's thoughts.

"That worked out well."

"Yes. He can have a boys' night out and we'll have a girls' night in. As soon as we get this sent."

They worked on the proposal until Amy was satisfied, and then emailed it to Sylvia.

"You want to order pizza?" Amy asked.

"Sure."

So they sat at the kitchen table eating pizza and chatted about everything from Amy's plans to redecorate the upstairs to Lauren's budding career to old times. The only thing they didn't talk about was the one thing they used to talk about most when they were young: boys.

Seth's name never came up in conversation. Neither did Jackson's.

Lauren was excited about this project. Sylvia had hinted that if it went well, there would be lots of other work coming her way.

She was also in the city with a set of keys burning a hole in her pocket. Since she was fairly certain she was going to be kept extremely busy for the next four weeks, she figured she'd better treat herself to a night of hot sex while she was waiting for the final go-ahead on Sylvia's project.

When Amy excused herself to go to the bathroom, Lauren pulled out her phone and sent a text.

12

SETH AND JACKSON usually got together once a week for a squash game and he was relieved that marriage hadn't interfered with their games.

He liked the total focus, the speed, the squeak of the ball skidding on the court. He and Seth were well matched so it was always a fight to the finish. This time he eked out a win, but he'd had to fight hard for every point.

After they'd showered, they settled in the lounge for a beer.

"You hear about Willy?" Seth asked.

"Do I want to?" Not that he didn't have a special fondness for their old schoolmate since his wedding-night prank had resulted in Jackson ending up in Lauren's bed, but the guy was a pratfall on legs.

"He got arrested."

Jackson almost choked on his beer. "What?"

Seth couldn't keep the grin off his face. "He went to a bar, see. Got shitfaced. Fell for the cocktail waitress and wouldn't leave her alone until she agreed to go out with him. She told him to pick her up the next day and gave him her address."

"She must be as dumb as he is."

"She would be if she'd given him her real address."

"Oh, I'm liking this girl."

"Yeah, so he's too drunk to realize he's got an address but no phone number. After they get kicked out of the bar because it's closing time, our boy genius decides to surprise the waitress. He shows up at somebody's place and starts banging on the door, screaming all the things he's going to do to this woman."

He knew Willy. He would not be cooing sweet nothings, but yelling crude suggestions. Also, Willy liked to sing when he was drunk. Loud, inappropriate songs. "Was there singing involved?"

"Probably. So the woman at the address calls the cops. They arrest him for lewd behavior or something. She also caught him peeing in her front yard so she decided to press charges."

"Ouch."

"Yep. Willy had to call in his dad."

"Double ouch." Willy's father was a famous criminal lawyer who would not have been thrilled by his son's antics.

"But there's a silver lining."

"I can't even imagine."

Seth leaned back, enjoying telling the story almost as much as Jackson was enjoying hearing it. "The story gets out on some blogs and the cocktail waitress tracks him down. I'm not implying that she's figured out he's a rich kid with a silver spoon. Maybe she fell in love with his mug shot—who knows? She tells him she made a mistake giving him the wrong address. The person whose bushes he peed in took a cash settlement and an apology, and his dad smoothed things over with the cops. Now Willy and the cocktail waitress are dating."

Jackson threw his head back and laughed, which started Seth off. They laughed so hard that other club members turned to stare. "Ain't love grand," he said when he could finally speak.

They toasted Willy. Drank some beer. "Speaking of love, how's married life treating you?" he asked.

Seth's humor faded. "It's okay. Takes some getting used to, I guess."

And a resounding advertisement for marriage that wasn't.

His text message alert sounded. Simple message. I'm in the city. Your place tonight?

His reply was instant and heartfelt. Yes.

"Some hot chick waiting for you?" Seth asked.

He grinned. "Totally."

"Lucky bastard." And the worst part was that the newly married man sounded as if he really was jealous of his single friend. What the hell was going on? He'd been sickeningly in love with Amy before the wedding. Now it sounded as though he might be having doubts.

Well, if he wanted to talk, Jackson guessed he would listen. And if Seth didn't want to talk about it, that was even better. Jackson had no idea what he could say, but he thought that if asked, he'd tell his friend to suck it up. A man didn't make promises to a woman and not try a little harder to keep them.

Luckily, they also had work to talk about and it was clear that now that Seth was a married man, his dad was giving him more responsibility in the firm. He hadn't come right out and said so, but Jackson had a pretty good idea that Amy and Seth's folks had bought them the townhouse. So why would a man who had a new bride, a new home and a rising career be jealous of a guy who worked for everything he got, had never had a girlfriend longer than a year and who, if he wanted to visit his family, had to go to a graveyard?

Amy wouldn't have been his choice, but ever since he'd met her, Seth had acted as if he was the luckiest man in the world. Now it seemed as if he wasn't so sure.

WHEN LAUREN LEFT Amy's place, Seth still wasn't home, but she could see Amy was ready for bed and she didn't want to stay any longer. Once again, she turned down an offer to stay the night and hugged Amy thanks.

Then she drew in a deep breath of the city on a summer night. Got into her car and headed for Jackson's place.

When she arrived at his building, she dealt with the front door and rode the elevator up to his apartment. All the time wondering what the hell she was doing. Even as she put the key into his lock.

The apartment was dark. Of course it was. If Seth wasn't home, Jackson wouldn't be. Maybe she should have headed to her own home first. It wasn't as if he was so eager to see her that he'd rushed home or anything.

She paused for a second wondering what to do, but he'd given her a key and asked her to stop by, obviously he wanted her to wait for him. She supposed she'd do as he'd suggested.

Get naked.

And wait.

But when she walked into Jackson's bedroom, even though it was dark, she knew he was there. His breathing was soft and slow, and she could smell him. She closed her eyes for a second, wondering when she'd learned his smell as intimately as she knew her own face in the mirror. Then she walked the rest of the way across the room and quietly stripped off her clothes, each movement feeling sexy and special, before she slipped into bed beside him.

When she wrapped herself around him, she found him also naked and warm from sleep. She kissed his chest first, then his belly, trailing her tongue down his buff, gorgeous abs. By the time she took him into her mouth, he was already hard. He'd woken and not made a sound or said a word.

As she pulled him into her mouth, he muttered something and reached for her, slipping a hand between her legs, teasing her, exciting her as much as she was him.

She licked and sucked him for a while, making sure he had a good head of steam going, enjoying the way his hips began to move with her rhythm, feeling the heat building in her own body.

Then she climbed to her knees and straddled him, grasping his hard cock, wet from her mouth, and rubbing it against her entrance, dragging this out for both of them before she slowly lowered herself onto him.

She sank down and stilled for a moment, savoring the pleasure of having him deep, all the way inside her body, of the feel of him stretching and filling her. His hands reached up, caressing her breasts.

"I wasn't sure you'd come," he said softly.

"I was at Amy and Seth's. I waited for him to get

home so I'd know you were here. But he wasn't home yet when I left. You guys really partied."

"What are you talking about? I've been here for two hours."

There was a moment when she suspected both of them were thinking the same thing. If Jackson had been home for two hours, where the hell was Seth?

"Maybe he got an emergency call at work."

"An emergency real estate call?"

Jackson shoved his hand through his sleep-messed hair. "I don't know. Maybe his folks needed him." He glanced at her. "You going to tell Amy?"

She shook her head. "Nothing good can come of me getting involved in their private business."

"Good. I have some private business that I'd like you to take care of."

She felt him smile in the dark, felt her own lips curve. Then she started to move and neither of them could speak.

She set the pace exactly as she liked it, changing the angle of her hips a little to increase her own pleasure, until she drove herself up to the first peak and over, tipping her head back as the force of her climax shook her.

She'd barely caught her breath before he pushed her back, raising himself, so they were face to face, legs crossed over each other's, open and equal.

She came again, crying out as she ground her pelvis against his, their bodies slick with sweat. They were both breathing hard. She collapsed onto her back and he followed her, still inside her, still hard as a rock.

She clung to him during the final moments of their mating, and he dipped his head and kissed her, so soft and sweet that she felt her breath catch in her throat.

They stayed tangled up, their harsh breathing filling the room. When they'd cooled down, she rested her palm lightly on the back of his hand where it was curled around her breast. "Amy worries that we don't like each other. She wants me to try harder."

He gazed at her through heavy-lidded eyes. "You try any harder and I may not survive."

She chuckled. "I'll leave your key when I go."

There was a moment's silence. "Keep it."

"But—"

"It's more convenient."

She felt suddenly out of her depth, as though the rules, such as they were, had changed without anyone telling her. "I wouldn't want to walk in on anything, you know, awkward."

He rolled over and gazed at her. "I told you I'm not seeing anyone else."

"But every woman I know thinks you're hot."

He was stroking her—long, sensuous movements of his hand down her breast, her belly and up again.

Three orgasms and she was heating up again.

"If I want my key back, I'll ask you."

He frowned suddenly and his stroking hand paused. "What?"

"Nothing much. You talking about the key made me think about tonight, with Seth. We were having a beer and your text came in. He asked if it was a hot girl and I said yes. He sounded really jealous. What's that about?"

"I don't know, but I don't like it. Did he mention going anywhere else after he left you?"

"No. He didn't say he wasn't going home, but I got the impression he was."

"I don't like this. I don't like it at all." Amy was her best friend. If her marriage was in trouble, then Lauren felt it was partly her burden, too.

"Hey. There are a hundred places he could have gone."

"I'm not going to tell Amy. I have nothing to tell. But I still don't like it. Name ten of the hundred places a married man might go to at ten o'clock on a week-night."

"I don't know. He could have gotten a flat tire. Maybe a friend called and needed help with something…"

"Maybe he got lost on the way home," she threw in. When he sent her a look, she said, "Just trying to be helpful. If it were any of those things, he'd have called Amy and let her know. You know what those two were like. They called each other or texted constantly."

"Don't remind me. Used to make me queasy the way they'd coo at each other."

"Now he doesn't even kiss her goodbye when he leaves the house."

"How could their marriage be going south already? They've only been at it a few weeks."

"Did you ever feel like Seth was sort of unrealistic where Amy was concerned?"

"Completely. No offense, I know she's your friend, but the way Seth used to talk about Amy, it was like she was the most amazing woman in the universe."

She nodded. "It was the same for her. He didn't even sound like a guy when she talked about him. More like a fantasy."

"You think they made each other up?"

"In a strange way, yeah, I do."

"And now that they're living together the fantasy's falling apart."

"Exactly. They are real people. And they are falling off the pedestals each of them built for the other."

He took in a big breath and let it out, which made her head rise and fall. After a while he said, "I've known Seth a long time. I don't think he'd screw around on her."

"I hope you're right. But where would he go, then?"

"How do I know? I can't ask him."

She felt suddenly irritated. "What is it with you rich, entitled kids? You all act like the world's a big, happy theme park and you've got a free pass."

His chest muscles went suddenly rigid and then she felt them relax. "Where did you get the idea that I'm rich and entitled?" She heard an edge of bitterness and wondered what she'd stumbled into.

"Come on, you went to boarding school with Seth and Willy and all the other rich boys."

"There are other reasons why a kid gets sent to boarding school. Trust me."

Again, she heard the undertone: bitterness, maybe some anger. What on earth? She noticed him glance across the room to where a photograph sat on his chest of drawers. He wasn't a man who filled his home with pictures and trophies. In fact, as far as she'd noticed, that framed photograph was the only one on display. It showed a much younger but identifiable Jackson with two people who had to be his parents.

She'd taken a peek earlier and thought that he looked a lot like his dad. Both had the same Irish good looks. In the picture, his father couldn't have been much older than Jackson was now and the resemblance was strong. His mother was a pretty, fresh-faced young woman who had an arm around each of her men and smiled happily at the camera. It was a photo like a million other family photos.

"What am I missing?" she asked softly.

For a moment, she thought he wouldn't answer, but finally he said, "Nothing. We weren't rich. My folks died. That's why I got sent to boarding school. Their life insurance paid for it."

There was a world of what was not said in his terse recital of the facts, and she felt immediately ashamed of herself for lumping him with Seth and Willy and the frat boys. "I'm so sorry," she said, having no idea what else to say.

"It's okay. It was almost twenty years ago. I don't want you thinking you're getting naked with a rich guy, because you're not."

In fact, she was getting naked with a guy she barely knew and didn't particularly like. She turned her head to look at him. "What are we doing?"

"Hell if I know," he answered, putting his lips to her shoulder. "But let's do it again."

He was obviously trying to lighten the mood, push away her sympathy and get them back to the easy, sex-only relationship they had going. She couldn't take away his bad memories, but she could give him the comfort of her body, which she gladly did.

13

WHEN SYLVIA CALLED Jackson and asked him to have an after-work drink with her, he didn't know what to say. She was terrific. Interesting, smart, attractive, and she lived here in the city, not miles out of town.

But there was Lauren.

And what was Lauren? They'd been honest that if either of them got serious about someone else, they'd end things. So why should he feel a stab of guilt when he agreed to meet Sylvia?

But he did agree and after work found himself on a patio in the sunshine while he enjoyed a beer and she sipped a glass of white wine. Sylvia was good company. Sharply dressed, easy to look at, smart and well-rounded.

After an hour or so of easy conversation, when their glasses were nearing empty, she leaned closer. "So, are you seeing anyone?"

He opened his mouth. Closed it. Was about to answer when she smiled and said, "Ah, a significant pause."

He grinned stupidly. "I'm not seeing someone exactly, it falls more into the 'it's complicated' zone."

She nodded. She didn't seem disappointed, more like a woman with little time to waste. He imagined a mental list with his name being crossed off and the next prospect moving to the top. "Well, if things ever become less complicated, give me a call." She rose, motioned for the check.

"Hey," he said, "I got it." Because it was the least he could do.

"Okay. Thanks. I'll see you soon."

He gave her time to get away before he left, then kicked himself for being a fool. Sylvia was amazing and he liked her a lot. He totally should have asked her out. He'd been honest with Lauren that he might and she'd been perfectly honest that she might start seeing Daniel. They were adults. No reason for anyone to feel jealous or get their feelings hurt so long as they were honest with each other.

He watched Sylvia as she opened the glass door and exited the restaurant, her hips swaying nicely.

He should run after her, tell her he was an idiot and ask her out to dinner. But he didn't. He waited for the bill. Paid it.

He knew why he didn't run after Sylvia. Because as terrific as she was, he didn't feel a sizzle in his blood when she was near.

He let out a breath. It was a nice summer evening. Maybe a drive to Napa would be a good idea.

He pulled out his phone and texted Lauren. What's up?

Her response came within minutes. Lunch with Amy and her mother.

Lunch? It was seven o'clock at night.

Her mother's birthday. Which apparently explained a lunch lasting longer than some people's workdays.

You in town?

Yup.

Excellent. Feel like getting naked?

With you?

He rolled his eyes. Seriously? Did she have to be like this even by text?

But he was already feeling aroused, knowing she was playing with him. He texted back, No. Sent it and then imagined her eyes widening as she read his response. He texted again. Me, and a bottle of massage oil.

Her reply was so fast he knew she'd been watching for his message. The masseur better be hot.

He is. And getting hotter by the second. View's great from my place. Come anytime.

She arrived within the hour looking more polished than she had the past few times he'd seen her. Her hair was up and her clothes a little more formal. As though reading his mind, she said, "Amy's mother took us to her country club."

He opened the fridge, pulled out a bottle of wine and poured two glasses.

"Thanks," she said, accepting one.

He had the music on low, balcony doors open so they could enjoy the view of the bay.

She fiddled with his TV remote and put it back

down again. She wasn't normally a fidgety person so he figured she had something on her mind.

Had she somehow found out about him having a drink with Sylvia? But if she had, all she had to do was ask him and he'd tell her there was no interest there. Until she did, he preferred to keep his slightly confused feelings to himself.

But she wasn't concerned about Sylvia, it seemed. She straightened a lampshade. Then said, "Have you told Seth about us? Well, not us, us, but this thing we're doing?"

"No." In truth, he might have, but Seth had never been known for discretion and he really didn't want this getting out. "You tell Amy?" Which was pretty much the same as telling Seth, only worse, since he'd get hassled for holding out on his best friend as well as for sleeping with the woman he was always dissing.

She glanced up at him. "No."

She couldn't seem to settle. She flitted, picking things up and putting them down. He didn't think she was taking an inventory of his crap, more that she was a tactile person who thought better when she touched things. "I thought about it," she finally said, "but…" She turned to him and he saw distress on her face. "It's different now. First, she'd tell Seth and then he'd probably tell the frat boys. And, I don't know, she doesn't seem like herself these days. She's been kind of tight-lipped and Amy never used to be tight-lipped."

"Maybe she thinks now that she's married she shouldn't be gossiping with her girlfriends."

She stared at him. "Jackson, she's still a woman."

"Right. I don't know, then."

"At lunch today her mother made some dumb remark about wanting to be a grandmother before she gets too old. I swear I thought Amy was going to start crying."

"You think whatever's going on with them is about kids?"

"No. No, I really don't. I know they talked all the time about how many kids they wanted and what their names would be. And they haven't been married long enough to be having problems conceiving. I think she's maybe having buyer's remorse."

He chuckled. "Buyer's remorse. I like that."

"Has Seth said anything?"

He shrugged. "I don't know. Last time I saw him, we didn't really talk about it, but it seemed like marriage wasn't as bright and shiny as he thought it would be." Plus he'd disappeared somewhere for a couple of hours.

She nodded slowly. "That's exactly how Amy is. When she used to talk about him he was like a movie star and a business genius and the world's greatest lover all rolled into one perfect package."

"I've known him for decades. Really, he isn't."

"I know that. But maybe she's only just figuring it out?"

"Yeah. Same with Seth, I guess. It must be tough when everything's gone so perfectly all your life, to find that there really is no perfect woman. It's like finding out there's no Santa Claus."

"I guess it's really none of my business, but I care about Amy. I want her to be happy."

He didn't think they could solve Seth and Amy's problems. That was up to the newlyweds themselves. Lauren was there in his apartment and he thought a couple of hot and sweaty rounds of sex would help calm her down, so he said, "Do you want me to be happy?"

His tone must have made it pretty clear where he was going, for her expression changed from worried to curious, to maybe a little turned on. "That depends on what makes you happy," she said, sassy, like the woman he'd grown to enjoy surprising.

"It would make me happy to see you over here, bent over this table, right now." He dragged his small dining table across the floor so it rested in front of the open doors of his balcony. He saw her breasts rise and fall as his words got through to her.

"Then it would make me happy to hike up that skirt and to spread those sexy legs."

She made a tiny sound, a cross between a gasp and a sigh.

"And then it's going to make me happy when I plunge inside you and take my sweet time until you cry out."

"You think I'm going to cry out?" Her eyes were getting that heavy look that made him hard and he could see her chest rising and falling as her breath grew more rapid.

"I do. I think you're going to yell out my name so loud they can hear you all over the Bay Area."

"Oh, you think so, do you?"

"I do."

She stuck her nose in the air. "I thought I was here for a massage."

"Oh, you'll get one. Later." He'd picked up a bottle of almond oil from the health food store on his way home. He had definite plans involving her naked body and massage oil. "Now, come on over here and bend over."

He thought he had her. She walked slowly toward

him, her hips swaying and a flush of excitement on her face. When she got to where he was standing, she said, "It's a good thing I'm not wearing any underwear."

And damn it, just like that, she took the upper hand.

LAUREN WAS SOLDERING two panes of leaded glass together when Amy called. She didn't have time to talk on the phone. When Sylvia's client had seen her sketches for the exterior windows, he'd been so thrilled he'd decided to add two extra interior doors in a complementary design to the commission. With the days counting down, she hardly had time to eat or sleep, let alone time to chitchat.

But it was Amy.

"Hey, what's up?"

"Did Sylvia tell you she and Jackson went on a date?"

A sharp, burning pain shot through her. "Ow," she yelled.

"What happened?"

"Burned myself. Sorry. What did you say?" She put her sore finger to her lips and sucked on the burned spot.

"Sylvia and Jackson went on a date."

"How do you know?"

"Because Sylvia told me. Well, she told me they were going. I never heard how it went, but they'd be such a cute couple, don't you think?"

"Adorable," she snarled.

"Look, you might hate his guts, but lots of women think he's pretty special."

"Then they can have him."

"Okay, grumpy cat. What's the matter?"

The problem was she felt a constant mild panic, sort of like incurable indigestion. "I'm screwed. That's what. When she's not out dating Jackson, Sylvia's adding more windows to the job and the repair took a lot longer than I thought. I've already cut down my hours as much as I can at the winery. I don't know what else to do."

"Can you hire some help?"

"I think the time it would take me to train them would cancel out any benefit."

"Anything I can do?"

She smiled. "No. But thanks for offering. I feel better knowing you're there."

"Are you eating?"

Who had time to eat? Never mind grocery shop. But she didn't need Amy swooping down to check on her like a mother hen. "Yes."

"Okay. You need anything, you call me."

"Will do." She tossed her phone aside and went back to work.

Her phone rang again seconds later. "I'll call you if I need anything," she said. Really, Amy was turning into her mother.

"But you haven't called," a British male voice said, sexy and teasing. "I sit here by the phone day after day and you never call."

She couldn't help but smile. "Daniel. Hi. How are you settling in?"

"San Francisco is a beautiful city. The work's interesting and I've found a nice apartment. I think I'm ready to start getting out a bit."

"Sounds like a good plan."

"I was hoping to take you to dinner next time you're in town."

She closed her eyes. Her finger was throbbing where

she'd burned it and all around her were the sketches and designs, the partly finished windows, the tools of her trade. Of course, one night out wouldn't kill her. In fact, it would probably be healthy for her, but the truth was she didn't want to date Daniel. She was aware of a small, mean impulse to go out with him, knowing that Amy would tell Seth and Seth would obviously tell Jackson. But she didn't have the time or mental energy for playing stupid games.

"I really appreciate the offer, but the truth is I've taken on a huge job. I barely have time to eat at all. I'm sorry."

"Not to worry. Perhaps another time."

"Yes. In a month or so. Thank you for calling."

"My pleasure. Take care." And he was gone.

So, Jackson had gone ahead and started dating Sylvia. That was fine. Great. Not as if she had time for him.

Her finger throbbed and her bad mood escalated. She had too much work on her plate, no help, and now she couldn't even indulge in uncomplicated sex. To add to it, she'd turned down a date with an interesting, attractive man.

Not that she had time for sex, no matter the level of complication.

A feeling thrummed deep in her gut—it was a strange kind of ache, as though she'd eaten something that didn't agree with her, like the time Amy had convinced her that extra chorizo on her burrito was really a good idea and that, no, those weren't the really hot peppers.

She didn't have time for a stomach ache. She rubbed her belly absently, but somehow she knew the pain wasn't from anything she'd eaten. Jackson and Sylvia. It was about Jackson and Sylvia.

Because Jackson and Sylvia meant no more Jackson and Lauren. Not that there'd ever officially been a Jackson and Lauren, but she'd started to think maybe there was more to Jackson than the frat-boy mentality and the I'm-God's-gift-to-the-women-of-California ego.

Little glimpses of a different kind of man had made her wonder if she could have been wrong about him.

She shook her head at her own foolishness.

It would have been nice for him to have told her he was dating Sylvia himself, though, as they'd agreed. Hearing the news from Amy made her feel like the last person to know what was going on in her own life.

She shook her head, did a few yoga stretches, determined to get back to her zone, and then went back to work. She tried to be philosophical. Men came and went, but she always had her work.

A week went by. She knew she'd never be able to sustain this pace forever, but for a month, she thought she could manage. If no disaster struck, the glass behaved and the Leonatos remained understanding, she'd make her deadline.

Once she'd completed a few windows, she emailed Sylvia to say she'd drop them off at the house. She knew she was being childish. A grown-up would call the woman who'd hired her for the project, but she didn't really want to talk to Sylvia. Besides, she couldn't find her phone.

Sylvia emailed back that it was great news and she'd arrange for the installer to come by the next day.

So, she shrouded her windows in padded blankets and placed them in her hatchback. Then she drove carefully into town, glancing fearfully into her rearview mirror, praying no one would rear-end her car.

It was Sylvia who opened the door and ushered her inside, where wonders were taking place. The old staircase had been moved and rebuilt, and walls had been taken out to open up the space. New flooring and lighting fixtures offered a modern look while still keeping the tone of the original house. "The house is really coming along, isn't it?" Sylvia said, as Lauren looked around her, and said, "Wow. It's gorgeous."

"I know."

Sylvia wasn't one for false modesty. She looked happy, glowing even, like a woman who was getting great sex.

"Place looks stunning," Lauren agreed, because it did. Sylvia was obviously a talented architect.

"I'm excited to see the windows."

Lauren brought them in one at a time, refusing Sylvia's offer to get one of the workmen to carry them. The possibility of a workman handling them carelessly—or, worse, tripping and breaking them—was too terrifying to contemplate. Once she had them inside the house, then they were Sylvia's responsibility. Until then, she preferred to handle them herself.

Sylvia studied each window with a critical and exacting eye. Lauren respected her business acumen and her high standards.

When she nodded and smiled, Lauren let out a breath. She had exacting standards, too, but it was still nice to know her work had been approved by someone else.

"I love what you've done. I could picture the windows from your sketches, but to see the actual colors really makes a difference."

"And when you get them installed and the natural light travels through them, that's when you'll get the full impact."

"I can't wait. I'm as excited as a kid at Christmas."

"You look great, by the way," Lauren couldn't help but remark. Sylvia had obviously had her hair recently styled and had that glow about her. In contrast, Lauren felt like a walking wreck. She needed more sleep and more exercise, and, looking at Sylvia, she felt as if she needed a few days' worth of personal grooming.

"Thanks." Then she grinned, woman to woman. "You know how it is when you start a new relationship? If I'm not at work or with him, I'm either at the salon or working out." She sighed. "Why are we women so hard on ourselves?"

"Heck if I know."

She wouldn't feel jealous. It was a petty, unbecoming emotion. So what if Sylvia was getting her hair layered and her body toned and polished for Jackson. It had nothing to do with Lauren.

Nothing.

She had more windows to finish and she couldn't lose sight of the deadline.

Sylvia might be headed to the gym, the spa and then a night of passion. Good for her. Lauren had to work.

14

JACKSON CHECKED HIS phone again. A frown dragged down his forehead as he contemplated the obvious. Lauren hadn't texted him back.

This was not the first time she hadn't responded. He'd been sending her Come on over, it's your lucky night type texts for a week now.

To no avail.

He'd even tried calling her, something he'd never done before.

He'd gotten her voice mail.

Fine. She didn't want to talk to him. He didn't have to be a rocket scientist to figure that out. So he went back to work.

Five minutes later, his cell phone indicated he had a text. He grabbed his phone so fast he almost knocked over his coffee, splashing hot black liquid on his thumb as he righted the cup. "Ow," he muttered, thinking of Lauren and the way she'd sucked her burned thumb at Amy and Seth's wedding.

But as it turned out, he'd burned his thumb for nothing. It wasn't Lauren. It was Seth, wanting to play squash after work.

Sure. Why not? Wasn't as if he had anywhere better to be.

Besides, maybe Seth knew what was up with Lauren.

After a miserable game, in which Seth beat him soundly, mocking him for not keeping his head in the game, they settled in for their usual post-game beer and catch up.

Of course, he couldn't come right out and ask if Lauren was okay, so he went for the subtle approach. He said, "So, are Lauren and Amy plotting to redecorate your house while you're out?"

Seth winced. He'd spent their last visit complaining that Amy was taking a house they'd both claimed they liked and redecorating every freakin' room.

"No. Amy joined a Pilates class. Haven't seen Lauren for a while. She's working on something."

Jackson tried to come up with something snarky to say, but without Lauren there to hear it, he couldn't summon the enthusiasm. Besides, he was worried about her. She worked all alone with dangerous substances. Hot guns and sharp glass. What if she'd hurt herself? A horrific vision of her needing help, trapped under a heavy piece of furniture that had fallen on her as she reached for her ringing cell phone, bloomed and wouldn't let go.

He scoffed at his own stupidity. Of course she was okay. But then why didn't she answer him?

"That woman sure is hard to please," Seth said.

"Amy?"

"No. Well, yeah, Amy's hard to please, but I meant Lauren." Seth shook his head. "Do you know those girls have a rating system for guys? One to ten. Lauren gave Daniel a seven."

"She was being generous."

"You're as bad as she is. I figure that guy's a catch. All that Britspeak the girls seem to love and he's rich and well connected. Has a great job."

"Plays polo," Jackson added.

"Exactly," Seth agreed, never one to pick up on subtle sarcasm. "And she gives him a seven."

"What did she rate me?" he asked before he could stop himself.

"I don't know. But Lauren told me that when Amy met me she said I was a ten."

"That's nice." In a slightly nauseating way.

"So Daniel called me looking for Sylvia's number."

"Sylvia? I thought he was interested in Lauren."

"He was. You saw him at our dinner. Totally into her. Amy and I were really excited. Thought they made a perfect couple. So, he calls and asks her to dinner and she blows him off."

"Well, he was only a seven." But a glow of satisfaction warmed him. He didn't want Lauren going out with a dick, and for some reason he'd decided Daniel was a dick with an accent.

"Yeah, well, don't sound so pleased with yourself. When he called and asked for Sylvia's number Amy checked with Sylvia, and she said sure, he should call her. Your Sylvia. And she said yes to another guy."

"She's not my Sylvia."

"Well, she could have been. You screwed up there, dude."

"She and Daniel will be perfect together."

They finished up their beer. "You want to grab some dinner?" Seth asked him.

"What about Amy? Won't she be expecting you home?"

Seth's jaw tightened. "Amy needs to get used to me having a life of my own. Some space."

"Sure, that's cool. I can't, though. I need to head back into the office for a couple of hours tonight. There's a bug I need to fix."

"Yeah, no worries. Maybe next week."

Jackson did go back to the office, mostly because he never wanted to lie to Seth. But he didn't stay long. He'd showered and shaved at the gym and was wearing clean jeans and a T-shirt. He hit the road. Even as he pointed his car north, he cursed himself for being such a fool. He and Lauren didn't have this kind of relationship. They were two very different people with nothing in common but amazing sex. A few miles into this strange, impulsive road trip, he called her from his car and left a voice mail. "Look, I know this is crazy, but I'm worried about you. You're not answering your phone, not responding to texts. If you don't want me to show up at your door, you'd better let me know, because I'm on my way."

As he drove, he realized that what he was doing was changing the nature of their relationship. If he got there and she was in bed with another guy, obviously it would be the end. He couldn't believe Lauren would do that to him, though. They'd been honest with each other and he trusted her to tell him if she was seeing someone.

Unless her not responding to his texts or calls was

her way of letting him know she was seeing someone. At least he knew it wasn't Daniel.

If there wasn't another guy in her life, then he hoped she was missing him as much as he missed her. There was no denying their chemistry. They were only compatible in one area of their lives, but damn, he'd never known anything like it. His body had grown accustomed to having her, and going without for more than a week had him feeling like an addict in withdrawal.

He chuckled as the dark road unrolled ahead of him. A sex addiction. Great. That was all he needed.

When the lights of Leonato Estate Winery rose ahead of him, he wavered once more. He wasn't a showing-up-on-the-doorstep kind of guy. He tried Lauren's cell phone one more time. Still nothing.

Okay, he thought, he'd swing by her place. If he could find her place. He knew she lived on a cottage on the winery estate because she'd told him so. He knew what car she drove because he'd seen it. Process of elimination should make it easy to find her, assuming her car was parked in front of her home. He'd hoped for a security guard who could warn Lauren he was on his way, but there wasn't one. A sign informed him he was on private property. He followed a lane behind the winery offices and the tasting room, to a scatter of more modest buildings.

A big house sat on a hill, and he assumed that was the home of the winery owners. But lower down were the scattered cottages. He cruised the lane and found Lauren's car. There wasn't a second car beside it, so he pulled up and parked. He climbed out and glanced around. Her cottage seemed dark. A quick look at his cell phone clock told him it was only 9:00 p.m. She couldn't be in bed yet.

He walked around and noticed a second building, more like a shed. Light spilled from it. Curious, he walked forward. Music spilled out along with the light. It made him think of Fitzgerald and the Charleston, jazz and flappers. Truly curious, he knocked on the door.

"DAMN IT, I don't have time for this," Lauren growled. She'd finished applying flux to the foil she'd folded over all the edges of glass for the current widow. Now she was ready to use the copper solder. Who would bang on her door? Unless it was the Leonatos complaining about the noise, which she doubted.

She went to the door and flung it open. She blinked when she saw Jackson standing there. "What are you doing here?"

At the same second, he said, "Are you okay? You look terrible."

For a stunned second, they both stared at each other. He broke the silence first. Wincing. "Not the first thing I meant to say to you. Sorry. But are you okay?"

"I'm working." She felt irritated at the very sight of him. How dare he arrive unannounced looking like a sex fantasy when she couldn't remember the last time she'd showered or slept. And he was seeing someone else.

"I tried to call," he said. "For a week, I've been texting and calling you." He shuffled his feet as if he felt foolish. "You didn't answer. I—oh, shoot me if you want to—I was worried."

She glanced around vaguely, trying really hard not

to be flattered that he'd worried about her. "I'm not sure where my phone is. I haven't seen it for days."

He could obviously see the chaos of creation behind her. "I caught you at a bad time."

"Did you drive all the way up from San Francisco?"

He looked slightly belligerent. "Yeah. Like I said, I was worried."

"Oh. Thank you."

She blinked her eyes a few times, realizing that she was going to strain her eyes if she wasn't careful. She had no idea what to say to Jackson. It was as though she'd been so immersed in her work that she'd forgotten her social skills.

He seemed as lost. The music was the only sound. Finally, he smiled and said, "Not what I'd have guessed your taste in music to be."

"I always play music that suits what I'm working on. These windows are for a house built in the 1920s. It helps if I play music of the period, especially when I'm designing, but I like to have it on when I'm constructing the window, too. Keeps me focused and authentic."

He frowned at her. "When did you last eat?"

"I don't know. What time is it?" Her stomach felt hollow, as if it had given up on reminding her to eat.

"It's after nine. At night." He grinned, as if she might have mixed up night and day. Which she probably could have.

"Oh. Um, I had breakfast." The remains of a container of yogurt and a spotted banana, the last of a bunch she'd bought last time she got groceries.

"Why don't I make you some dinner?"

Dinner would be amazing. A break would be amazing. "I don't think I have any food in the house."

He sent her that charming grin once more, the smile of a man who was getting enough sleep and bathing regularly and had seen the sun in recent days. "I lived in poverty as a student. Trust me, I can make a meal from pretty much anything."

"I need half an hour," she said, knowing she had to get the window pieces put together.

"You come when you're ready."

She turned to her work. Then back to him. "Thanks."

"Do I need a key to get into your place?"

"No. Door's open."

And just like that, he was gone.

WHEN SHE WALKED into the cottage, the most incredible smells assailed her. She entered the kitchen feeling as though she'd walked into a dream. Jackson stood in front of her stove, stirring something that smelled amazing, like an authentic Italian restaurant. Her senses sprang to life and she realized she was starving.

"How on earth did you manage that?" Had he brought food with him?

"Let's see. A can of tomato paste in the back of that cupboard there." He pointed to where she kept canned goods. "Some bacon in the freezer. A can of olives. You've got lots of dry spices, and I took the liberty of opening a bottle of wine."

Thank goodness the Leonatos always kept her well stocked with wine.

"You don't have garlic, or parmesan, or bread, but there was half a packet of spaghetti. We'll make do."

She felt, as her senses reengaged, that she couldn't sit down to dinner in the clothes she'd been working in all day. "Can I grab a quick shower?"

"Sure." She thought she caught a hint of relief in his tone.

When she caught sight of herself in the bathroom mirror, she understood why. Was that really her? Her hair was dragged back from her face in a ponytail that hung limp. Her eyes were shadowed from lack of sleep and she was wearing the worst of her work clothes. They hung from her frame, so she was pretty sure she'd lost weight.

She threw herself into the shower, shampooed her hair twice, soaped herself all over and then, after drying swiftly, slapped some of the expensive body lotion on her skin. She didn't have time for makeup or to dry her hair, but at least she was clean. She ran a comb through her wet hair, brushed her teeth, scooped up her dirty clothes and changed into a comfy pair of jeans and a blue cotton sweater that was one of her favorites.

When she returned to the kitchen, Jackson popped the pasta into boiling water. She loved that he'd timed dinner for her convenience. Then he passed her a glass of red wine.

She raised her glass in a silent toast and then sipped.

She was about to set the table when she saw he'd already done so. As she scanned the empty fruit bowl, the breadless bread bin, she said, "I don't normally live like this."

"I didn't think so."

She rolled her stiff neck. Suddenly, Jackson was behind her, his strong hands kneading the knots in her neck and shoulders. She pressed her lips together to keep from moaning with pleasure. The touch of his fingers on her skin, the feel of him right there behind her, made her quiver in parts that hadn't quivered in too long. She realized she wasn't only starving for food.

Then she frowned. "Wait. Does Sylvia know you're here?"

His hands paused, then continued their magic. "Sylvia? No."

She felt fuzzy. Going too long without proper nutrition or sleep was making her stupid. "But you're seeing her."

"No, I'm not."

"You went out for dinner together. Amy said so."

He moved, taking his lovely massaging hands with him, so he was in front of her, where she could see his face. "We had a drink after work. That was it. I think she's seeing Daniel."

"Daniel? English Daniel? But—" She shut up before she sounded like a twit, boasting that Daniel had asked her out and she'd turned him down.

But Jackson did the crinkly-eyed thing that always made her knees weak. "He asked you out?"

She nodded.

"You turn him down?"

She paused, and then nodded again. "I'm too busy to date," she explained.

"Oh."

The humor of the situation started to hit her. "What did you tell Sylvia?"

He paused and turned back to the stove. Finally, he said, "I told her that it's complicated."

She didn't know what to say to that since she strongly suspected that she was the one complicating his life. "So they turned to each other. It's kind of perfect, don't you think?"

"I do. I hope it works out for them."

He drained the spaghetti and spooned the sauce, and she thought how capable he was. Who knew he could cook?

When she took her first bite, she thought nothing had ever tasted so good. The flavors exploded in her mouth and she had to force herself to take her time, not to gobble down her meal like a starving person.

It was quiet. He hadn't put on music and after the noise of her workshop, she was grateful for the silence. "How was your week?" she asked.

Normally they didn't talk about personal stuff. But he'd driven all the way out here to check on her. He'd cooked her dinner. She felt as though something had shifted and taking an interest in his life was okay.

He blinked, as though as surprised as she was that she'd asked him about his work. "It was good. We're beta-testing part of the site. How about you? Tell me about the commission."

So she did. Explaining her concept, and how the job had grown during the week to a much bigger project than she'd envisioned. "That's why I'm so slammed."

"Maybe you need help."

She wrinkled her nose. "I'm not good at asking for help."

He smiled. "I can see that." Then he leaned forward. "I need to work tomorrow, but there's nothing planned for the weekend that I can't blow off. How about I come back tomorrow night. I'll cook for you. Then I'll help out over the weekend. I can lift heavy things, keep you fed and watered. What do you think?"

What did she think? She sipped her wine, pondering. One: the way her heart leaped when he offered to spend the weekend with her made her a little nervous. She'd believed he was no longer available to her. That he was seeing Sylvia. Now it turned out he'd missed her enough to drive up here and they were back on again. Two: if he got in her way and kept interrupting her, she'd be worse off than she was now. Three: if he was as good as his word, this weekend could make the difference between stressed success and relaxed success, since failing to complete such a prestigious commission on time was not an option.

She put down her wineglass. "Here's the deal. If it works, you stay. If you slow me down or get in the way, you go. Fair?"

"Fair."

"And thanks."

He rose, took their empty dishes to the sink. She got up to help him, but he waved her away. "You need to rest. I'll wash up."

"It's a long drive back," she said, walking behind him and wrapping her arms around him. He felt solid, warm, sexy.

"It is," he agreed.

"Maybe you should stay."

"You want me to?"

More than she wanted the earth to keep turning. "Yes."

"Okay. Go slip into nothing and I'll be there in a minute."

15

LAUREN WOKE SLOWLY, stretching luxuriously. As she came to full consciousness, she was fairly certain there was a smile on her face. Mmm. If ever a woman had needed the release of a couple of rounds of great sex, she was that woman and last night had been the night.

As she rolled over, she noticed that she was alone in bed. She stretched once more and got out of bed. It was just after seven and she felt fantastic, inspired, ready to face the day.

When she wandered into the kitchen, she found a scrawled note in the middle of the counter, a red-and-green apple holding down the corner like a paperweight. Beside it was a granola bar. The note said, "Remember to eat. See you tonight. J."

As love letters went, it didn't rate all that high, but she was certain that apple and the granola bar hadn't come from her kitchen. He must have had them in his car, leftover from a lunch or a trip to the market.

She bit into the apple and found it crisp and sweet. Just like Jackson.

As she brewed coffee, she thought about how she

was letting him into her home, her life. Letting him help her this weekend. Seemed to her that this suggested they were moving beyond casual sex to some kind of a relationship. The notion scared her a bit—they were so different, understood each other so rarely. And yet...

Something about the two of them together worked. Maybe it wouldn't work forever, but it was working for now.

Anyhow, she didn't have time to think about her personal life. Not now, not when her professional life was taking over every waking minute. She'd see how the weekend went, if he even showed up as he'd said he would, and then after it was over she'd worry about the future. Feeling good about things, she finished her apple and then pulled on some old work clothes.

Her coffee ready, she took it with her out to the workshop. And she got to work.

WHAT KIND OF WOMAN got so obsessed by work that she ran out of food? Jackson shook his head as he walked around the market with a shopping cart. He'd taken a quick stock of her kitchen supplies when he'd blearily stumbled out of bed, knowing he needed to get a really early start if he wanted to shower at home and get to work on time.

As he'd taken stock, he'd quickly realized it would be easier to make a list of what she did have than what she didn't. Lots of coffee. That was good. She liked a dark brew, and kept a few pounds of beans in the freezer. She had spices, and a few random cans of food, and her wine cellar was well stocked, but mostly her cupboards were bare.

He threw eggs, bread, cheese, fruit and vegetables into the cart. He had no idea what kind of cereal she liked, so he bought a couple of varieties. He bought steaks for dinner tonight, the fixings for Caesar salad and baked potatoes, and chicken for Saturday night. He smiled at his own domesticity as he planned wraps for lunch on Saturday and tuna salad sandwiches for Sunday.

All day, he'd alternately relived the passion they'd shared and worried about Lauren. Which was crazy. She wasn't his girlfriend. She wasn't his problem.

And yet he knew all about the drive to succeed because he recognized it so well. How many times had he run himself almost as ragged working on programing for a client deadline? Too many to count. Why should he be shocked that she worked as hard as he did? He supposed he'd always thought she was soft, pampered like Amy was. But the woman he'd seen last night hadn't seemed soft or pampered. She'd looked very much like a woman who needed some pampering, and that had spoken to him on a level he understood only too well.

He was shocked to find that he wanted to make her life a little easier, to smooth her path. Well, he'd messed up their easy, uncomplicated, sex-only relationship for good. And he wasn't sure how he felt about that. Whether it would turn out to be good or bad, he doubted they could ever go back now.

And maybe he didn't want to.

As he stood in line to pay, he tried to imagine the sharp-tongued Lauren as his official girlfriend. He winced at the picture in his head of them arguing their entire lives away.

He arrived at Lauren's place just before eight that night, with a car full of food and a hastily packed bag of clothes and toiletries.

Her place was as dark as it had been the night before. He knew exactly where he'd find her, could picture her working in her studio, but decided not to bother her. Instead, he let himself into the unlocked cottage, flipped on lights and put the potatoes on to bake even before he unloaded the food. He was hungry and imagined she would be, too. He had no idea what she'd eaten, apart from the apple and granola bar he'd left her—all he'd been able to find in his car—but he doubted it had been much.

Once the potatoes were in the oven, the steaks marinating and the salad prepared, he walked over to the workshop. He knocked, but when a minute went by with no answer even though he could hear jazz playing, he opened the door and walked in.

Looking at a woman when she had no idea she was being observed was so different from looking at the same woman when you were engaged in conversation or she was simply aware of your gaze. Lauren was completely absorbed in what she was doing. She held a stick of lead in one hand and the hot gun in the other and she was bent forward beading solder and then using the gun like a precise paintbrush to spread the liquid metal.

The window she was working on was stunning. There was no other word for it. Even without light streaming through it, he could see the patterns and shapes, the colors. Her face was a study in concentration, her shoulders held high in a way he instinctively knew meant knotted muscles from too many hours bent forward in the same position.

She wore an old denim shirt, baggy jeans that hung on her slim frame and boots.

Tenderness washed over him, along with a desire to ease her life somehow. He frowned. He didn't want to feel warm emotions, didn't like the way he'd worried about her all day, wanted to feed her and rub her shoulders. When had this fun sex thing turned serious? How had Lauren, of all women, squeezed past his defenses?

As he stood there, it occurred to him that he'd never bothered with defenses when she was around because he'd assumed her sharp tongue had made him immune.

Fool that he was. Not only was he not remotely immune to her, he was half in love with her.

He gulped as the unwelcome thought hit him. Half in love? Hell, no. Where Lauren was concerned, he'd never done anything by half measures, whether sparring or making love or falling for her. He wasn't half in love with her. He was all-the-way, head-over-heels, going-under-for-the-third-time-and-watching-his-life-rush-in-front-of-his-eyes in love with her.

Did he move? Did he howl like an animal trying to chew its own leg off to get away? Did she feel his intense gaze on her? He didn't know, only that she stilled in her work and then slowly raised her gaze until they were staring at each other. For a second, no one moved, spoke, so much as changed expression. He felt the intensity of her gaze, the ball of barely acknowledged emotion pressing against his chest. Truth was it felt more like a panic attack than love.

He didn't want to be in love with Lauren. He wanted to run far and fast.

But he didn't. He stepped forward and said, "Didn't want to disturb you."

"How long were you standing there?" She hadn't liked him watching her without her knowing it.

"A few seconds." A few deadly seconds, enough time for him to realize he was in love with her. He took another step forward. "How's it going?"

She shrugged, and then rolled her shoulders, both irritable and tight-muscled. "Slower than I want it to go. I planned to finish this window tonight." Her tone suggested that was no longer a possibility.

Well, he couldn't work miracles, but he could offer her what he had. "What can I do?"

She looked confused, as though unsure what he could do. He didn't blame her. He'd never made a window. "I'm not sure. I don't usually have help."

"There must be something simple and tedious that I could do for you."

She nodded suddenly. Decisive. "Think you can handle masking tape?"

He grinned. "I practically have a PhD in masking tape."

"Okay." She grabbed his hand. Took him to a second wooden table. "See these pieces of glass?" They were neatly stacked, smaller ones in boxes. They looked like collections of sparkling puzzle pieces.

"Yep."

She grabbed a roll of tracing paper and laid it on the work bench. On it was a drawing, clearly of the window. "It's to scale. You want to get the pieces, a section at a time, and fit them together. Once you've got the first section done, call me, and I'll start foiling while you put the next section together."

He had no idea what foiling was, but figured it wasn't important at this stage. "I think I can handle it."

"Cool. Let me know if you have any trouble."

She stood for a second, watching, and he realized that she was waiting for him to prove himself. "Lot of pressure," he said, realizing that she'd scrawled initials on the page that he had to assume represented colors. He began to pick up pieces, place them on the paper. After a couple of minutes, she patted him on the shoulder and went back to what she was doing.

They worked like that, in silence, for maybe thirty minutes. He could smell the burning metal of the solder, hear the sexy wail of the music. For someone who worked all day long, day after day, on computer codes and possibilities, a virtual world of the future instead of the real one of the here and now, it was refreshing to work with his hands, knowing that what he helped Lauren build would end up gracing someone's house, lending it a beauty and functionality that would last well into the future.

He hadn't slept a lot last night, had driven to San Francisco and back again, worked a full day, shopped for food, and yet the tiredness he'd felt melted away as he chose colored glass puzzle pieces and fitted them together according to her design.

On the page, a stylized tulip with an art deco flair began to take shape. He could see that there were panels in the door, each of which would have a similar look, but not an identical one. Interesting.

She touched his shoulder, and he was so immersed in what he was doing that he jumped. He turned to look at her, and she nodded, looking pleased. "You got it. That's exactly it."

"Now what?"

"Now we tape."

They ripped masking tape into inch-long strips to hold the pieces of glass in place. Once that was done, he said again, "Now what?"

"Now we take a break. I'm starving." She kissed him lightly on the lips, a casual little smacker that felt more intimate than some of the things they'd done naked.

"I'll go throw the steaks on." And rescue the potatoes.

"Steak, wow."

"I'm building your strength for later," he teased, and they walked back to her cottage.

Since she didn't have a barbecue, he grilled the steaks in the oven. They drank water because they were going back to work afterward. He suspected that drinking alcohol was not conducive to working with hot irons and glass.

"Tell me everything that's been going on," she said as she stabbed into the salad he'd made. "I feel like I've been on vacation in some non-English-speaking country. I have no idea what's going on in the world."

"The world's still pretty much a mess," he warned her. "No worse or better than a week ago."

"How about our friends? What's the gossip?"

"I don't really—oh, I know, did you hear about Willy?"

"No. I've barely spoken to Amy."

So he told her about Willy, and she laughed as hard as he had when he got to the part where Willy was dating the cocktail waitress who'd inadvertently got him arrested. "I love it," she said. "It's karmic payback for him and the frat boys tricking us into spending the night together."

"Biggest favor they ever did me," he said before he could stop himself.

Lauren's eyes widened and she stared at him for a moment. Then she grinned, a sexy, teasing grin. "I agree."

Maybe she thought he meant only that he was grateful for the sex. Maybe that was good.

After they ate, they went back to the shed. She finished the window she'd been working on when he got there, and he felt that he was helping her get ahead on the next one. It was a good feeling.

It was after eleven when they called it quits. Lauren was yawning hugely as they got to her bedroom. "I was going to shower again, but I'm too tired."

"Me, too."

They stripped and fell into bed, and he rolled her up against him.

"Thank you," she said, her big eyes serious as she gazed at him.

"You're welcome." He kissed her softly on the lips.

She snuggled up against him. "Do you mind if we don't...you know? I am just so tired."

"No. Go to sleep." And strangely, as he held her in his arms and felt her soft, deep breathing, he didn't mind that they hadn't had sex. He felt calm, content, more right than he'd felt in a long time.

He fell asleep with the feel of her soft, warm skin against him.

16

As a stress reliever, great sex was right up there. But, Lauren discovered as she woke the next morning, feeling rested and alert, that simply sleeping beside Jackson all night even without the sex had done almost as good a job.

She smelled coffee and smiled. Dragged on her nightshirt and padded out to the kitchen.

Okay, maybe it wasn't simply sleeping beside him that had lowered her stress level to the high end of normal instead of dangerously high—it was the way Jackson had come through for her.

Because of him, she'd eaten properly. He'd also helped her with her commission. To her surprise, he'd caught on right away and she'd trusted him. There was food in the house, and the smell of coffee drew her to the kitchen the way honey drew bears.

"Hi," he said, when she entered the kitchen. He looked all morning sexy with a little stubble and mussed hair, wearing a T-shirt and shorts.

"You made coffee."

"Which I think was very big of me since you didn't put out last night."

She giggled, and really, she'd never thought of herself as the giggling type, but he was so adorable and she felt a tiny bit shy. Everything was changing between them and it seemed as if it was all happening too fast. Or was nothing changing and she was reading way too much into his simple kindness? She'd never been any good at judging what men meant when they did things. Usually, she asked Amy, but since Jackson was still a big secret, she couldn't even ask her best friend.

"I'm sorry about that. I can't believe I fell asleep. Maybe I can make it up to you later?" He'd mentioned staying for the whole weekend, but she didn't want to hold him to it. It was a sunny Saturday and he probably had a hundred things he could be doing.

He rose and got out one of her blue pottery coffee mugs, having headed unerringly to the correct cupboard as though he lived there. Then he poured a dark stream of coffee. She could tell it was strong, the way she liked it. "You take milk or sugar?"

"Never."

He nodded as though she'd given the correct answer. She glanced at his own half-empty mug and saw he drank his black, as well. One thing they had in common, then.

As he passed her the coffee, she thanked him and sipped gratefully.

This morning, everything felt new and possible. How had she come to this? It was only a few weeks ago that she'd thought Jackson was an entitled ass. Now she found he had a soft side. He could cook, he'd cared enough to drive a long way to make sure she was okay.

He'd done all that and then hadn't pressured her for sex when she'd crawled into bed bone tired.

What kind of man did all that?

A good man. The kind of man a girl could seriously fall for if she wasn't careful.

"I thought I'd whip up one of my world-famous omelets," he told her.

"You make world-famous omelets?"

"Well, my world is pretty small."

She smiled, walked over to him and kissed his too-gorgeous face. "I should tell you a secret," she said.

His eyes immediately went cloudy, a sign that he was getting aroused. She loved that she could do that to him so easily. "Yeah? What's your secret?"

"Omelets make me seriously hot."

"Then I'll put extra eggs in yours."

He rubbed his lips back and forth over hers. All the sexual buzz she'd been too tired to act on last night came roaring at her. Fast and hard.

"You do that. In fact, I'll help you. It'll go faster."

Had she ever cooked breakfast with a man before? She didn't think so. There'd been times where she and her ex had both tried to make toast or get cereal in the morning, and one or the other might have made brunch for the other, but working together like this was ridiculously intimate and kind of fun.

She grated cheese and chopped some spinach, while he diced mushrooms, beat eggs and heated her heavy frying pan. While he made the omelet with the casual flair of a TV chef, she took care of making toast and setting the table.

"There's orange juice in the fridge," he told her.

Of course there was. She felt as though she'd fallen

asleep at her workshop table and was dreaming all of this. But the smells were too real, the sizzle in her blood too visceral.

She was as awake as it got.

"You're right," she said, after taking her first bite of the fluffy, perfectly cooked omelet. "This is a world-class dish. Did you learn to cook so you could impress women?" She was teasing, but not completely.

"I learned to cook so I could survive on my own," he countered. He chewed and swallowed. "But impressing women is a nice side benefit."

"Tell me you're handy around the house and I'll call the wedding planner," she said.

When his gaze connected with hers, all dark blue and sexy, she almost couldn't breathe. "I can fix anything."

She reached across with her bare foot under the table and rubbed his calf. "Good, because I have something that needs fixing."

He sipped his orange juice and seemed to contemplate her request. "Is it electrical?"

Was he kidding? The electricity shooting between them was probably going to cause a fire. "Yes, it's electrical."

Her foot stroked higher and found his thigh, warm and a little hairy. She felt his breathing change. "I'm also good with plumbing."

"Plumbing could be involved."

"I'm really good with my hands." As he said the words, he slipped one hand under the table and began to track warm fingers up her leg.

"I could definitely use a handyman." Her voice didn't even sound like hers. More like something you'd hear on a nine-hundred number. She wasn't putting it on—the lust flowing through her had clearly gone to her vocal cords.

He pushed his chair back so suddenly her foot fell to the floor. He came around, hauled her out of her chair and kissed her fast and hard.

A moaning sound came from her mouth and she threw herself against him, kissing him, plastering her body to his. With an arm, he pushed their plates to the back of the table, where it met the wall, and then he hoisted her up so she was sitting on the edge. Her nightshirt was shoved up over her hips. He pulled her to him and pushed all the way in in one long thrust.

She was so wet, he slid easily inside her, and they started to move—crazy, uncoordinated, all need and heat. The table banged against the wall and something fell to the floor with a crash. A piece of cutlery, she thought dimly and then she couldn't think at all.

She clung, wrapping her legs around him, leaning back on her hands so she could gain some traction and push up against him, meeting him thrust for thrust. They were both panting. He reached forward and pulled the neck of her nightshirt down so her breasts were exposed and he could touch them, play with them. As her passion built she heard herself making crazy sounds, heard him making some crazy sounds of his own.

When she thought she'd climb out of her skin with wanting, he slipped a hand between them, rubbing her hot spot in time to their thrusts.

Oh, it was so good. Too good. She couldn't hold out. The dishes were banging together, the table hitting the wall, skin slapping against skin, all of it mixing with their mingled sighs and whispers.

"Oh, yes," she moaned.

"You make me crazy."

"Good." She liked him crazy. She liked them both crazy with lust and wanting and this fire that died down but was never quenched.

And then she couldn't hold back anymore. She felt the wave build, rise and crest as her body ground against his, and her head fell back on a long, heartfelt cry of release.

He was right there with her, and held her until they were both spent. "I think I put my hand in the butter," she said, pressing her forehead to his hot, sweaty chest.

"Come on. Let's get you in the shower."

And somehow, under the streaming, steaming water, they took each other again. More slowly this time. The water pounded down like warm rain, or tears, and something frighteningly sweet began to unfurl inside her.

She didn't want to think about what it might be.

She had too much at stake to go soft on a guy. Not now. Not with Jackson. So, she took her pleasure, gave him his and then climbed out and grabbed a towel, all business now.

"I need to get to work. Stop distracting me."

He slapped her bare butt as he walked past her and into the bedroom. "Can't help it. You're impossible to resist."

Then he pulled on old clothes he'd brought with him in a sports-type duffel bag, and she dug out her own. Then they headed out to her studio for another day's work.

"Does it feel like a Gershwin day?" she asked, scanning through her player for suitable tunes.

"Why not?"

They worked together but not together for a few hours, and she found he was great to have around.

At noon he told her he was going to make lunch. "And if you're not in the kitchen in half an hour, I will come and get you and drag you out to eat."

"I'll be there."

He made her lunch, wraps with cheese and avocado and lettuce, not seeming to mind at all that he was giving up an entire weekend to look after her. When they'd finished the wraps he'd made, she said, "Look, this isn't fair on you. You work all week and this is your time off. Please, go out. Do something fun."

His smile was a little twisted when he answered. "It is fun for me, spending time with you. Besides, I'm learning how to make a stained-glass window. I had no idea."

"At least get out for a walk or a run or something. Get some air."

"I wouldn't mind a run," he admitted. "And I need to get a few things at the market, things I forgot for tonight's dinner."

"I am so going to come over and do something nice for you when this is over," she said, blown away by all he was doing for her.

"Get back to work. I'll be back in a couple of hours."

"Sounds good." She kissed him goodbye before heading back to work. Then she realized what she'd done. She'd kissed a man goodbye she was going to see again in a couple of hours. She stalked out to her studio faster than she needed to, realizing she was starting to act like Amy used to act with Seth. What was she doing?

She'd imagined it would be a relief to have her studio back to herself for a few hours, but the truth was she missed having Jackson there. He wasn't an annoying presence, asking her things every five seconds or trying to talk to her whenever a thought flicked through his brain. He had the same kind of focus that she did. He took whatever task she gave him and got right into it. If he asked a question, it was an intelligent one.

She'd come to enjoy having him working in her space, watching the way he handled the glass as though he might smash it to pieces if he wasn't careful, how he'd picked up the basic skills pretty fast. He hadn't been kidding when he'd told her he was good with his hands.

If she'd learned one thing, it was that she might be able to stand having a helper next time she needed one. She'd have to keep that in mind.

She was deep into a tricky bit of repair work when she heard banging on the door. She wondered why Jackson didn't simply walk in, then thought maybe his hands were full. She started to fantasize about takeout cappuccinos. When she flung the door open, her jaw dropped.

"Amy! What are you doing here?"

"I came to see if you're still alive."

"Of course I am."

"Good. Then you can take a break for thirty minutes and have some lunch."

"You drove all this way to bring me lunch?"

"I tried to call, but you're not answering your phone. I figured you were lost to the world."

"I can't find my phone. I put it somewhere." She glanced around her vaguely, but no phone jumped out at her. "I already had lunch."

"And here I thought you were working yourself to the bone, forgetting to eat or sleep or brush your hair." Amy sounded a tiny bit peeved and Lauren didn't blame her. She'd come a long way to rescue someone who didn't need rescuing.

Only because she was a day too late, but Lauren didn't share that fact with her.

Phone. Where the hell was her phone?

"Maybe you could call me again and I'll see if I can find my phone."

"If you didn't hear me calling before, why would you hear it now?"

"I'll turn off the music."

She cut off Ella Fitzgerald in midcroon and Amy pulled out her phone and hit speed dial. A tiny sound came from somewhere in her studio. It took a few minutes and a few more calls, but she finally unearthed the thing. It was wedged between an old window frame and a roll of masking tape.

"Found it," she said brightly, holding up the phone.

"Come on. I drove all this way, least you can do is make me some tea."

"Sure. We can sit outside. I can take a break."

Amy looked summer pretty in a white jean skirt and a floral top. Her Italian sandals showed off a new pedicure, and her hair and makeup were flawless. When she moved her hands, her wedding ring sparkled in the sun.

Lauren didn't quite know what bothered her. Perhaps it was that Amy looked almost too well turned out for a casual Saturday.

Amy stopped at her car and pulled out two big bags of stuff. When Lauren opened the door for her, she walked them in and plopped them both on the counter, then glanced around in amazement. She opened the fridge door and peeked inside. "You have food."

It was true. The fruit bowl was heaped with healthy fruit, the fridge contained plenty of produce and Jackson had stocked her cupboards with all sorts of dry goods.

Amy turned to her, seeming confused and a little put out. "I thought I was on a mercy mission. You didn't answer your phone and I pictured you working yourself to the bone and not finding time to buy fresh food. I guess I was wrong."

She couldn't go on lying to her best friend. Not now that Amy had really gone out of her way to be a good friend bringing food and checking up on her. She took a deep breath. "Actually," she said, "you're not wrong."

As she spoke, Amy started rustling in the paper sacks on the counter, digging out deli sandwiches and cookies. She'd even brought chocolate. When she emerged, she said, "What did you say?" But before Lauren could repeat herself and get started on her confession, Amy was speaking again. "I didn't only come here to bring you food. It was kind of an excuse. I really needed to get away."

Lauren moved behind her friend to put on the kettle. It seemed like a tea kind of talk was about to occur. "Why? What happened?"

"Seth forgot our anniversary," Amy said in a clipped, disappointed tone.

She knew she'd been working too hard and maybe her social skills were already rusting, but unless she'd also been in a time warp, she was missing something. "You've only been married a few weeks."

"Not our wedding anniversary!" Amy exploded. "The anniversary of our first date."

"Oh." Lauren had never understood why people celebrated every relationship marker, but Amy and Seth had always celebrated the day they first met and then the day of their first date. She didn't realize the tradition was supposed to continue once she and Seth were married. Kind of seemed as though Seth hadn't realized it, either.

"Do you mind if I use your washroom? I drank two coffees on the way up."

"No, of course not." She couldn't remember what toiletries Jackson had left in her bathroom, but she'd decided to tell Amy about him anyway. However, she didn't want him to come barging in while Amy was in the midst of talking about her marital troubles so she quickly texted him. Amy's here. I'll text you when the coast is clear.

When Amy returned, she fully expected an inquisition, but it seemed as though either Jackson had hidden all traces of his presence in her home or Amy was too preoccupied with her missed anniversary to notice anything else.

Lauren brewed tea and Amy unwrapped sandwiches.

Not even for her best friend could Lauren eat a second lunch. "I already ate lunch. I'm so sorry. I didn't know you were coming."

Amy regarded the sandwiches, and then rewrapped

them. She grabbed the cookies and the box of Ghirardelli. "Screw it. Life's short. We'll skip straight to dessert."

So, they sat outside in the shade of a grape arbor at a small round table. The vineyards stretched in all directions, the vines green and laden with young grapes.

As they sipped tea and munched on cookies, Lauren said, "It's not only that he forgot the anniversary of your first date, is it?"

Amy shook her head, looking miserable. "I don't know what to do. We're still getting wedding presents and I'm wondering if I've made a terrible mistake."

"No. I'm sure you're not. You love Seth and he loves you."

"I thought so, too. We were so perfect together. But since we've been married, I'm seeing a side to him I don't like."

"I'm sure there's an adjustment period."

"I guess. But—" her face started to pinch "—I think he might be having an affair."

"What? Already?" Then realizing that was a completely tactless thing to say, Lauren continued, "I mean you've only been married six weeks. How could he possibly be having an affair?"

"I don't know. But he's out a lot. And when he comes home late and I ask him where he's been, he gets really cagey. The other night he told me he was working late, but I'd already driven by his office and his car wasn't there. Why would he lie to me unless he has something to hide?"

Lauren did not like the sound of that. And she'd been a witness to the night that he'd disappeared for a couple of hours after playing squash with Jackson. "Did you confront him?"

"Of course I did. He started yelling at me and said I didn't trust him. Then he went out and slammed the door in my face." She shoved a chocolate in her mouth. "And I keep eating because I'm upset, which is making me fat."

"You're not fat." She nibbled a cookie, thinking. "Have you thought about marriage counseling?"

"Who goes to marriage counseling after six weeks of being married? It's so humiliating. My parents paid a fortune for the wedding and both of our folks helped us buy the townhouse. If they found out we're having problems already, they'd kill us."

"I'm sure they wouldn't. Anyway, why would they find out?"

"Because, if we started going to counseling, Seth would blab to his dad. They work together and he tells his dad everything."

And Amy was as much of a blabbermouth with her own mother.

"You have to do something."

"I am. I'm making sure I always look my best and I bought some new lingerie, and I've been reading books on how to improve our sex life."

"Is it working?"

"Not really. The sex used to be so good between us. Now sometimes he says he's too tired."

She thought of how she'd been last night and how understanding Jackson had been. She said, "Maybe he really is too tired. You told me he's got more responsibility now at work. What if you—I don't know—just kissed him good-night when he's tired."

"It was so much better before we got married. If we were together, we both looked nice and we'd go out to nice places and we'd have sex. And when we were tired, we both went home to our own places."

"Maybe you should have kept your apartment," Lauren said. She was joking, but Amy looked at her seriously.

"Maybe I should have."

They talked for a while longer, but Lauren didn't know what to say or how to help.

Amy stood up. "Well, I'd better get going. You've got work to do. But thanks for listening. I really needed to talk to you."

"Of course. Anytime."

They hugged.

"Don't forget the housewarming party next Saturday."

"You're still having it?" With the marital crisis going on, she'd assumed they'd drop the idea.

"Of course we're still having it. A lot of the same people will be there that were at the wedding. I'm hoping that when we're reminded of how special our wedding was, we'll get the spark back again."

"I hope it works." Though privately she thought that any spark that could die out in six weeks probably wasn't much of a spark to begin with.

When Amy drove away, Lauren stood for a moment, gazing after her. Hoping it would all turn out okay.

Then she texted Jackson that the coast was clear.

He arrived about ten minutes later, wearing running shorts and a technical shirt. She took a moment to admire his athlete's build.

He grabbed a paper sack of groceries out of his car and must have caught her expression. "What?"

"People keep showing up at my house and donating food. I'm starting to feel like the food bank."

"Amy brought food?"

"She did. Also chocolates."

"Damn," he said. "I forgot the chocolates."

They walked into the kitchen together. "I'm so sorry you had to stay away. I had no idea Amy was coming over."

"I felt like Clint Eastwood in *Bridges of Madison County.* Waiting for the busybody tea lady to leave so I could come back and screw my girl."

"You watched *The Bridges of Madison County?*"

He shot her a sheepish grin. "The woman I was with at the time wanted to see it."

"Of course she did. Well, much as I'd love to drag you to my bedroom now, the tea party is over. I need to get back to work."

"Did she set your work back very much? You've got a sort of tense expression on your face."

"No. It's not that." She glanced at him. "Seth keeps disappearing. She's worried he's having an affair."

"Seth?" He shook his head. "Seth's not that kind of guy. Anyway, he's crazy about Amy and they've been married, what? A month? Two months? They're practically still on their honeymoon." He unpacked his food sack and added things to her full fridge.

"Except I get the feeling the honeymoon ended before the wedding." She held up a hand. "Don't say it."

He turned to look at her. "Say what?"

She pitched her voice low and imitated him. "'Never

getting married.' It's what you say every time there's something about Seth and Amy that you don't like."

"I wasn't going to say that. I think marriage can work. With the right person."

He turned and headed out the door toward the studio. She was so stunned she stared at his retreating back for a moment before following him out.

17

"Tell me the housewarming is canceled," Jackson said as he laid foil around the edges of one of the cut pieces. They'd fallen into a pretty efficient routine. He helped with everything except the cutting, the glass grinding and the soldering, all of which she preferred to do herself. But he was adept and had quickly caught on. He also worked long hours without complaint. She had to admit she wouldn't be half as far along if he hadn't given her his time this weekend.

"I asked Amy that, too. No. It's going ahead."

"What is it with these people? Their marriage might be over before it starts and they still have parties?"

"She thought it would bring them closer."

"Ha. Remember the antipasto plate?"

"I know. But after that they did okay."

He cut another section of foil. "Is this another deal where we bring a present?"

"I'm not sure. I think so."

"What are they going to do with all that stuff if they break up?"

"What are they going to do with it all if they don't?

Did you see all the wedding gifts? Plus the shower gifts and then there's all the shopping Amy's been doing. They'll need a bigger place for all their stuff."

"What are you getting them?"

"I thought I'd give them one of my wine coolers. I know I make them, but Seth's always said he'd like one."

"That's a great gift. It's personal. Something you actually made. I'll probably go online and see if there's anything left at the gift registry they don't already have."

"Too bad you can't buy marriage counseling. That's the gift they need."

They worked together the rest of the weekend. By Sunday evening, she looked around the studio at window after window, ready to deliver. She threw her arms out and turned in circles. "I can't believe it. I'm not only going to make my deadline, I'll have these to Sylvia early."

Jackson watched her, a sleepy smile on his face. "Good."

She walked over and threw her arms around him. "Are you staying tonight?" She knew he had to get back to work and had wondered if he'd leave today, but he hadn't mentioned anything and she didn't feel she had the right to ask.

"I was planning on staying over. That okay with you?"

"Oh, it's more than okay. I'd like to take you to dinner tonight to thank you. Well, there's no way I can ever thank you enough. But I'd like to take you to dinner." He'd come through for her. No one in her life had ever come through in this way except for Amy. It was thrilling and scary. She didn't want to rely on anyone. Never had. But he'd been there when she'd needed someone, without being asked. He'd stepped up.

She could seriously fall for a guy like that.

He gazed down at her all sexy and rumpled. A ragged square of masking tape was stuck to his T-shirt and she was pretty sure there was a bit of foil sparkling in his hair like a tiny halo. "Are you asking me out on a date?"

A flutter of panic flapped crazily in her chest. "No, no. It's not a date. It's a thank-you dinner."

"Then I accept." He pulled her in for a kiss. "And, FYI, if it was a date, I'd still say yes."

What did you say to someone who insisted on changing the rules in the middle of the game? She had no idea, so she kissed him back. Seemed the simplest thing to do.

She tidied the studio, made a mental plan of what she needed to do the following day and then happily left to take a well-deserved break.

The sun was afternoon heavy. She could smell the dirt of the fields, felt the growing green in the vines and grapes. With so much work accomplished, plus good food and great sex, it was tough not to feel pretty good about life.

Jackson seemed pretty content, too, for a guy who'd given up a precious weekend to be a chef and stained-glass apprentice.

"Do we need to get dressed up?" he asked. "Because I didn't bring anything fancy with me."

"No. I know a casual bistro where the food is great. Wear whatever you like."

So, he wore the same jeans he'd driven down in with

a black polo shirt, and she wore her good jeans and a peasant blouse that made her feel feminine and relaxed. She slipped her feet into sandals and brushed her hair until it shone, then left it loose around her shoulders. She took a little extra time with her makeup and added big hoop earrings.

When he saw her, his eyes warmed. Even the way he looked at her made her quiver.

She tried to ignore the inconvenient conviction that was growing in her, the idea that this no-strings-attached, sex-only, never-see-the-light-of-day affair was getting pretty stringy, involving a lot more than sex, and encroaching on daylight hours.

Was that a problem?

She suspected it was.

But she refused to worry about the future when the present was so delicious. Tomorrow would take care of itself.

He drove and she directed him to a little bistro she liked. The storefront entrance was nothing fancy, and the interior was brick walls decorated with old posters and a bizarre collection of antiques, from a warming pan to an old miner's pick. The open kitchen and rough wooden tables added to the casual air.

The waitress greeted her by name and seated them at one of the prime tables by the window. The restaurant was pretty full for a Sunday night, a mixture of tourists and locals. The buzz of conversation reminded her how isolated she'd been for the past couple of weeks.

They ordered a bottle of local wine that the waitress recommended, which was good enough for Lauren, and decided to share fresh mussels and a salad with wild greens and goat cheese. She chose trout for her main meal while he went with a lamb shank.

The ordering done, they found themselves sitting across a small table looking at each other. It was the reason they'd never done this before. They were great in bed. They'd never been great in a social situation.

She twiddled her hair.

He took refuge in sipping his wine.

They'd spent all weekend together; how come they didn't have much to say to each other? Then again, all weekend they'd been focused on work. Their conversation had mainly revolved around him asking her how to do things and her showing him.

He glanced up and caught her gaze. Smiled in a slightly panicked way.

Oh, the hell with it. "Is this weird?" she asked him.

He contemplated the question. "It's not that I don't have things to say, more like I don't know how to talk to you."

She sipped her own wine, amazed he so easily grasped the same thing that was bothering her. "Yes!" she cried eagerly. "It's like we're so good at dissing each other that I'm scared if I say something that you'll misunderstand me or bite my head off."

He nodded. Seemed to study the problem.

After a moment, he said, "I have an idea."

She thought his idea might be to get back in the car and make a break for it, but it wasn't. He said, "What if we agree not to say anything rude or unkind to each other. Hold back the snark."

"What? Ever?" As if that was possible.

"No." He scoffed at the idea. "I mean tonight. For one

meal. We won't spar or argue. If you speak, I will listen and try to return the conversational ball like an adult."

"Okay." She liked where this was going. "And if you say something, even if I think it's stupid and deserves a put-down, I'll hold my tongue."

"Well, that's a start."

"All right."

At that moment, their mussels arrived so they had a brief reprieve as they speared their shellfish and dipped their bread into the luscious broth. "You were right," he said. "This place is fantastic."

She could have remarked that he'd eaten only one mussel and it was too early to call Zagat, but she refrained. Understood that he was approving her choice. "I thought you'd like it," she said instead.

After that, it seemed easy and much more natural. Even though she kept reminding herself this was a thank-you dinner and not a date, it was pretty hard to hold on to that notion since they were going to go home to bed together. It seemed as if the line between thank you and romantic had been crossed.

By the time the salad came, the wine bottle was half-empty and she felt bold enough to ask him what she'd wanted to ask him since he'd told her his parents were dead. Sure, she could have asked Amy, almost had when she'd shown up for tea, but an odd protectiveness had hit her. She didn't want to gossip about Jackson and his past behind his back. She wanted Jackson to tell her his story himself.

Knowing it was probably difficult for him, she started slowly. "I didn't know you'd lost your parents. I'm so sorry."

"You thought I was a pompous rich kid choking on my sterling silver spoon."

"I did," she admitted.

"Now you know I'm not."

"Actually, I don't know anything but what you've told me."

He stabbed a piece of goat cheese and some greens onto his fork. A candied pecan rolled onto the table and he picked it up and popped it in his mouth. "That's not much," he said, and pushed the forkful of salad into his mouth.

"No. It's not. I—I guess I want to hear your story."

He chewed. Swallowed. Sent her a half humorous, half serious look. "Kind of veering into dating territory, aren't you?"

She was. But she didn't care. "I think our enemies-with-benefits program went out the window when you showed up with food and helped me all weekend."

"Do you wish I hadn't?" The humor was gone. He was all serious now.

A funny kind of ache started in her belly. She wanted this to be real and she was frightened of it being real all at the same time. "No. I am really glad you came."

"Okay, then. So am I."

She ate some salad. Helped herself to more bread. Busied herself so he might feel inclined to speak if he wanted to.

Finally, he did.

"My parents were great. I don't think I had any idea how lucky I was until later. We were—" he shrugged "—happy. I know my folks would have liked more kids. I think that was the only sadness, but they were good people. We lived in Maine. My dad was a fire-fighter. Mom was a part-time bookkeeper. We didn't have a lot of money, but when you're a kid you don't know or care about stuff like that."

He put down his knife and fork. Gazed into his wine with a frown forming on his face. "It was a stupid, stupid accident. It was snowing badly. I was staying over at a friend's and they came to get me the next morning." He swallowed. "Fresh snow over black ice, a sharp bend in the road, a semi coming in the other direction. They never knew what hit them. At least that's what I tell myself."

"Oh, Jackson. I'm so sorry." And in her head she thought, *Poor, poor little boy.*

"Yeah. It pretty much sucked. My grandparents had to take me. I hardly knew them. They were my mom's folks and I'd barely seen them. They lived here in California. They had their own lives, no idea what to do with a twelve-year-old kid. There was some money from the life insurance. They used it to stick me in boarding school. They probably thought they were doing the best for me, sending me to a good school where I'd be with other boys."

"You were newly orphaned and they shipped you off to boarding school?"

"It was a shit time. Until I met Seth."

She wondered how anyone could take a boy who had just lost his parents and send him off to a school where he didn't know anyone.

He gazed at her, a faint smile on his lips. "You might not think Seth is the world's greatest guy, but he was a good friend to me when I didn't have any. You don't forget something like that."

"No. You don't."

"And that's why most of my friends are rich, entitled guys and I'm poor. I work for everything I get and I'm fine with that. But there's no giant inheritance coming, no trust fund."

"I was so wrong about you."

"I'm thinking I was wrong about you, too."

Her lips twitched. "That depends what you thought."

"Pretty much what you thought about me. That you and Amy were best friends because you went to the same debutante parties and your mothers played tennis at the same club."

She chuckled and then she laughed so hard she choked. "What a pair of snobs we are."

"Snobs?"

"Well, reverse snobs. Both dissing the other for being rich when, in fact, we're both poor."

"I thought your stained glass was a hobby." He paused. "Until this weekend."

"Now you know."

"What's your story?"

"Nothing as tragic as yours. Divorce. My mom bitter and renting the former pool house of rich people. They live next door to Amy. I used to hear Mom and Dad arguing on the phone. She said he didn't take me often enough."

"Ouch."

"Yeah. He has another family. I almost never see him."

"And your mom?"

"She worked hard. Resented the way her life turned out, I think. Mostly, I hung out at Amy's. I love my mother and she did the best she could, but honestly, it was Amy's parents who mostly brought me up. My mother married again and she's a lot happier now."

"But the damage is done."

She was pleased that he understood so well and yet his words had been matter-of-fact, not gushing with sympathy. "Yeah."

"So, you think we might have been wrong about each other?"

"Yeah. I think maybe." She contemplated how very wrong she'd been and how much she was enjoying getting to know the real Jackson. "You did nothing to make me see the truth."

He acknowledged that with a nod. "Neither did you."

"True." She'd enjoyed poking away at his entitlement, believing his good looks were salon and gym induced. Now she knew better. He put running shoes on every morning and he ran. He had a chin-up bar in his apartment and she suspected he did sit-ups and push-ups on the rug while watching TV. As for the salon looks, now that she'd spent time with him, she realized he spent the minimum amount of time on grooming. His looks were a gift from nature. "This changes everything."

"Oh, I hope so." He sounded so sincere that for a second she was shocked, and again that warm, hopeful feeling began to bloom inside her.

When they got home that night, the mood continued. They made love and it was different from ever before. It wasn't a lighthearted romp promising physical release and nothing more. This was so much deeper and more real. She felt that she was making love with every part of her, letting him see and have all of her.

It was the most exhilarating experience of her life. Possibly the most frightening.

She felt, every time their gazes connected, that he was feeling the same way, that he was opening to her in a way that was as difficult for him as it was for her. They'd both always been so careful, she was certain, not to open themselves up to hurt. No wonder they'd sparred and tormented each other. It was so much easier than facing the fact that they were more alike than different.

Maybe she had recognized their kinship on some deep level and it had frightened her. For, in Jackson, she knew she'd found someone who could really see and understand her.

To open herself like this, to let him in, a woman would have to be very careful or she could find herself... Oh, no. She wasn't. Couldn't be. Not with Jackson.

Not in love with Jackson.

But he touched her and her body responded. He kissed her and her world seemed right. He entered her body and she felt as though she was a part of him and he was a part of her.

He was deep inside her. They were locked together, moving as though they could climb right into each other's skin. When the deep tremors began to rock her, she felt the trembling spread everywhere, so intense was the pleasure.

And then she was coming, and he was coming and the moment was so exquisite she almost couldn't breathe.

She kissed him, putting everything she felt but wasn't able to say into that kiss. When they turned to sleep, his hand cupped her breast, close to her heart.

18

MONDAY MORNING DAWNED, ridiculously bright and sunny, even by California standards. When she padded out of the bedroom to the kitchen in search of coffee, she found another of the J notes. This was as sentimental and keepsake-worthy as the last. It said, "Last night was incredible. I'll call you. J." Yep, that was a letter to tie in blue ribbon and keep forever. Still, she touched her fingertip to the *J* and pictured him driving back to town through the dawn.

She missed him already, she thought, as she put fresh coffee on to brew.

And that was the trouble with love. You got caught up in emotions that didn't used to trouble you. Like missing a man when he wasn't around, thinking about him when you should focus on work, wondering if he was thinking about you. *Oh, just stop it!*

She didn't throw away his note, though. She left it on the counter, where she could see it. And she made certain her phone was charged as she carried it with her to her studio.

It was wonderful to walk in and see the progress

they'd made over the weekend. On impulse, she called
Sylvia and offered to bring the next set of windows by
the next day. Sylvia expressed delight at her progress.
And, since Sylvia was with Daniel and not Jackson,
Lauren was able to chat with the architect with per-
fect friendliness.

They agreed to meet at the house Tuesday afternoon. Lauren put down her fresh mug of coffee and
pulled out her portable music player. She ran through
possibilities and went back to Gershwin. So what if it
reminded her of Jackson? As the first notes of "Sum-
mertime" filled her studio, she reflected that she was
a woman who had blundered into love with a man,
without ever intending to. Gershwin understood that
kind of blunder.

Then she got to work, letting the glow she had ac-
quired from her dinner and that amazing lovemaking
last night float her along. It wasn't distracting, this
warm feeling; it was good. She'd always been so afraid
of love, fearing she'd end up dependent, bitter, maybe
both. Now she saw that she wasn't her mother. Love
with the right man was both liberating and creative.
Her work had never felt so inspired. She made tiny
changes as she was working, seeing new possibilities
in everything.

The phone rang and she dropped her cutters. Damn.
She grabbed her cell and discovered it was a marketing
call. Cursing, she put it down and got back to work.

No one else called. Not once.

In the whole day.

He'd said he'd call. Every time she found herself in
the kitchen, there was the note, telling her in black and
white that he was going to call.

He didn't.

Finally, she crumpled the note and pitched it in the trash.

JACKSON PICKED UP the phone. Put it down again. He was starting to act pathetic. He'd shown up, unannounced, walked into Lauren's house and taken over. Okay, he really felt he'd done her a favor, but had he come across too strong?

Something magic had happened over the weekend. He couldn't stop thinking about how great Lauren was and how right it felt being with her. But she was skittish. He'd seen something that looked very much like fear in her eyes when they'd grown closer over the weekend.

There were moments when he'd wanted to tell her how he felt. While they'd been making love, he'd almost blurted out the fateful words he could never take back. But she wasn't ready. He could see that she wasn't.

As he'd driven back this morning, he'd had time to think and he'd realized that what the woman needed was a little space. He couldn't push her or rush her, or she might panic and run.

At least, that's what he thought she'd do, since it was what he did himself if a woman tried to get too close to him too fast.

He'd be cool. Give her a day or two. Then he'd call. Keep it casual. See if she wanted to get together. Maybe he'd drive up later in the week.

He wanted to ask her if she'd go with him to Seth and Amy's housewarming and that was a big step. He knew what he was asking. For her to show up with him in public, in front of the very people who were most important in their lives. That would be a statement.

Oh, they'd take some heat, showing up holding hands like the lovers they were after all the sniping and sparring they'd done, having convinced all of their friends and especially each other that they hated each other.

He grinned at the picture in his head. He could take it.

In fact, he looked forward to showing up with Lauren on his arm. She was, he was beginning to realize, the best thing that had ever happened to him.

He just needed to be very careful not to screw it up or he could lose her. He'd never had counseling after his parents were killed, but he was beginning to realize that the reason he'd never had a girlfriend longer than a year, the reason he pushed women away when they got too close, was that he was terrified of loving and losing again.

Now that he'd fallen in love with Lauren, he was determined to do everything he could to treat her carefully. He recognized that she was like him. She was as scared of getting hurt as he was. Maybe more so. He'd take it easy. Go slowly. Ease her into the idea of them as a couple.

So, he refrained from calling her as much as he wanted to. He'd left a stupid-ass note. That was bad enough. She needed a little space so she could see he could love her without needing to be with her 24/7.

He could love her.

And if the world was a just and decent place, she could love him back.

He simply needed to play his cards carefully and it could all work out.

He focused on work. Went for a run after his day was done. Wondered how Lauren was doing and once more resisted the urge to call her.

Play it cool, he reminded himself. He thought Tuesday evening would be the time. She would have had a couple of days to work uninterrupted, and maybe she'd want to talk to him. He liked the idea of a casual after-work phone call. He might feel her out, see if she was open to the idea of going to Seth and Amy's house-warming together.

He then spent a fruitless hour online. Seth and Amy already owned pretty much everything they'd asked for in their wedding gift registry. There were a few items remaining, but he could not call himself a man and show up to their place with silver pickle forks.

His fingers itched to call Lauren. First, because she might have some ideas on what he could get. Second, because he really had to tell someone about the pickle forks.

Somehow, while he was on the gift registry site, he ended up in the jewelry section. How could there possibly be that many styles of engagement rings? He scanned solitaires, cluster rings, rings that featured a colored stone, like an emerald or a sapphire or a ruby, surrounded by diamonds.

A woman who worked with stained glass might like a colored stone. He pictured her with a ruby, thought it would suit her coloring. When he found himself seriously picturing his ring on her finger, he knew he'd made a fool of himself big-time. How many times had he told her he was never getting married?

And now he couldn't imagine not marrying her.

How he'd gone from pickle forks to engagement rings, he'd never know, but he knew which one he'd rather buy. As for Seth and Amy, they had a fancy wine fridge installed in their kitchen. He supposed a couple of decent bottles would be as good a gift as anything. At least he could show up with wine and still feel manly. Of course, wine made him think of Napa, and that made him think of Lauren.

He was tired enough from the weekend and the early morning that he'd assumed he'd sleep like the dead. But, in fact, when he got into bed it felt cold. A little lonely.

He'd only spent a weekend with the woman. How could he miss her in his bed so keenly?

Punching the pillow didn't help. Deep breathing didn't help. In the end he flipped on the TV and watched a twenty-four-hour news channel for a while. Then he flipped to a golf game. That was slow moving enough that he ought to fall asleep.

The phone woke him. He was disoriented at first, wondering who was in his bedroom talking, then realized he'd fallen asleep with the TV on. He flipped it off even as he grabbed his cell phone, a smile chasing away his sleepiness. He knew who was calling. Who but Lauren would phone him at 5:30 in the morning? Who else knew he was usually up this early? He'd been right not to push her. Now she was calling him.

"Morning, gorgeous," he said into the phone. "I missed you last night."

Silence greeted him and he had the sinking sensation that it wasn't Lauren on the phone. He hadn't even bothered to look at call display, fool that he was. "Jackson, it's Amy."

He sat up, suddenly alert, his heart thudding as visions of car wrecks slammed him. For he heard panic in her voice, and that could only mean disaster. And for him, disaster would always present itself first as a car wreck. "What's wrong with Seth?" He needed to know the worst right away.

"I don't know," she wailed. "I was hoping he was with you."

He rubbed a hand across his face. If Seth had lied to Amy and said they were together, then he needed to tread carefully. Oh, he'd pound Seth senseless when he caught up to him, but there was a code involved here. "When did you last see him?"

"Last night! He said you two were playing squash and then he never came home."

"You tried his cell?"

"Of course I tried his cell. He's not answering." Her voice rose, a combination of fury and panic. "If he's not with you, then where the hell is he?"

The code only went so far. If Seth was in trouble or sick or in the hospital or something, he wouldn't help his friend by lying. "He's not here."

"Oh, God. What if something's happened to him?"

What if he's sound asleep in the arms of another woman?

"I'm calling the police."

"No. Don't do that. Not yet." The last thing he wanted was for Seth to be humiliated. For his father, also his employer, to find out…whatever there was to find out. And at this point, it was nothing. "Look. If he was in trouble or in the hospital or something, you'd know. He has ID on him. Someone would have called you."

"What if he was mugged? Or murdered? And his wallet and ID were stolen? And there's no one to identify him."

He spoke soothingly. "Here's what I want you to do. Make some tea. Try to stay calm. Keep your phone with you in case he calls. I'm going to start calling Seth's buddies. What do you bet he ran into an old friend on his way home and stopped off for a few drinks? You know what a lightweight he is. He's probably passed out somewhere and he'd be super embarrassed if you made a big fuss."

"But what about work? What will I say if his father calls?"

"Maybe, if it's his dad, don't answer the phone. Look, I'll get right on this. We've got a few hours. I bet he crawls home soon, hungover and sorry for himself."

"You really think so?"

"Yes." At least he hoped so.

He dragged himself out of bed, wished for a shower and plodded to the kitchen, where he put coffee on. Then he tried to think. If he were Seth, where would he go?

The fact that he'd lied about where he was going last night seemed pretty suspicious, but Seth was not a devious guy. At least he never had been. Jackson would have sworn that Seth was the last man to have an affair, especially when he'd been so crazy about Amy. But if he wasn't with another woman, then where the hell was he? And where had he been all night?

He picked up the phone. He'd call Seth. That seemed

the best place to start. Maybe he hadn't picked up when Amy called because he knew he was in deep shit. But for his old buddy? If Seth was in any shape to answer the phone, Jackson had to believe he'd answer to him.

He barely had the phone in his hand when his intercom buzzer went.

He was across the room in a second. "Yeah."

"It's Seth."

"Thank God. Come on up."

When Seth arrived he looked awful. Pale, rumpled, scared. He wore athletic shorts and a shirt suitable for playing squash, which pissed Jackson off. He didn't want to be the guy's alibi.

The second he walked in, Seth said, "You have to help me. Tell Amy I was here all night."

"Sorry, dude. She already called."

Seth lost all the color in his face. He was unshaven, bleary eyed and his usually styled hair was a mess. His clothes were creased. As though he'd slept in them. "I told her I was with you."

"I know. That's why she called here."

The coffee was ready so he turned back to his galley kitchen and poured two mugs of strong coffee. He figured they both needed it. Seth's hand shook a little as he picked up his mug with a muttered, "Thanks."

"I covered for you for last night. I let her believe we'd played squash, but I couldn't lie and say you were here all night. What if you were really in trouble?"

"No. You're right. I get it." He looked up at Jackson with appeal. "I don't know what to do."

"First thing you'd better do is call your wife. She's

worried sick. I think I talked her out of calling the cops, but I'm not sure."

Seth grabbed his phone. Stood looking at it. "I don't know what to tell her."

19

THE RINGING PHONE dragged Lauren out of a very nice dream. She blinked sleepily. Wow. Her first night without Jackson beside her in bed, and she'd dreamed about him. A very hot dream. Her clock told her it was just after five-thirty. She only knew one person who got up that early. She rolled over, feeling sexy and wonderful. She picked up the phone. "You'd better have a good excuse for calling me so early. I was having the best dream."

"Lauren, it's me," a very panicked, very female voice cried.

Okay, not Jackson. She sat up knowing that Amy calling her this early could not be good news. "What is it?"

"Seth never came home last night." And then her best friend, the person she'd loved like a sister for the better part of two decades, burst into tears. "I don't know what to do. He's been acting so strange and then last night he went to play squash with Jackson and he never came home."

"Did you call Jackson?"

"Yes. Seth's not there. Jackson said not to panic, he's going to try and find Seth, but I can't stand it. I'm climbing out of my skin. What if he's dead or in the hospital with amnesia?" She caught herself on a sob. "Or what if he's with another woman?"

"Don't move." She was already throwing her legs out of bed. "I'm on my way." She doubted very much that Seth had amnesia, unless it was the kind of amnesia where you forgot you were married.

"Should I call the police?"

She considered that for a second. "No. Not yet. If he's in some kind of trouble, you'll get a call."

"That's what Jackson said, too."

"Well, two smart people can't be wrong. Try not to worry. I'll be there as fast as I can."

"Thank you."

As she stuffed herself into clothes, and grabbed her bag and phone, Lauren had never so regretted living an hour's drive away from her best friend. And that was if the traffic cooperated.

She drove as fast as she dared, pausing only once to hit a drive-through coffee shop to buy a venti dark roast to keep her awake.

When she arrived at Amy and Seth's, she got out of her car and paused. If there was some kind of marital crisis going on between them, she had to be careful sticking herself in the middle. Her job was to support Amy. She had to remember that, even though she was so angry with Seth she could belt him one.

It was six forty-five in the morning. Lights were on in most of the houses in the neighborhood. A BMW pulled out from the driveway next door and a guy in a suit sent her a curious stare. Well, if she didn't want to get arrested for vagrancy, she'd better move.

After taking a deep fortifying breath, she headed for the front door.

She knocked and less than a minute later, Amy opened the door. She looked awful. Tearstained and frightened and angry. Her usually perfect hair was a mess, her pajamas splattered with coffee.

Lauren opened her arms and Amy fell into them. "Thank you for coming. I don't know what I'd do without you."

"I'm always here for you. Like you are for me."

"I know."

"Have you heard from him?"

"Yeah. He hardly said anything, only that he was on his way."

"Well, that's good, right? He's not in the morgue or the hospital."

Amy didn't look as relieved as she might have. "Which narrows down the possibilities of where he was all night. I'm voting for he was with another woman."

If there were a polling booth, Lauren would be ticking the yes box on that one, too.

"Before he shows up, why don't you wash your face and put on some clothes? You'll feel a lot better not facing him in your pajamas."

Her eyes widened. "You're right. I was so upset I spilled my coffee all over myself."

"I'll make you some fresh coffee while you get dressed. Then I'm going. This is between the two of you."

"No. Please don't go. I need you here for support. If that rat bastard's sleeping with someone else, then out he goes. I'm serious. You know what I've been doing since he called?"

Packing his things would be her first guess.

"Searching the internet for divorce lawyers."

"Well, don't make any calls yet. Now go get dressed."

As she brewed coffee in the fancy new machine in the fancy new kitchen in the fancy new house, she wondered what was going to happen. Maybe Seth wouldn't have been her choice, but he was Amy's. And he'd hurt her best friend. She wanted to take the gleaming, razor-sharp carving knife out of the fancy new carving set and shred Seth into ribbons for wrecking Amy's dream marriage.

Amy was back almost as soon as the coffee was ready. If she didn't look her usual self, she looked a lot better in a pair of black trousers and a black top. Her face was pale without makeup, but she'd brushed her hair. In all that black she looked as though she were going to a funeral. Maybe that was the point.

While they drank coffee, Amy ranted. And Lauren, like a good friend, listened.

Before long, they heard the front door open and slam shut. Lauren reached over and laid her hand on Amy's forearm. "Before you start yelling, hear what he has to say."

Amy pressed her lips together hard and nodded.

Seth walked into the kitchen looking pale and scared. He wore some kind of tennis outfit, which made him look like a truant schoolkid. To Lauren's surprise, Jackson was with him.

Their gazes caught and she felt her heart bump against her ribs. He gave her the ghost of a smile, and then turned to Amy, who was glaring at her husband without saying a word. "I'm here because Seth asked me to come in with him, but you say the word and I'm out of here."

"Me, too," she agreed. Fervently hoping the newly-weds would give them both the boot.

But both of them shook their heads.

There was silence. Seth didn't even sit down. He stood there, looking foolish and lost. Amy continued to glare. Lauren had no idea what to do. Jackson took charge. "I say, let's all get some coffee and take this into the living room."

"Don't you have to go to work?" she asked him.

He shook his head. "I called in. Took the day off."

She nodded, recognizing that she'd likely be taking the day off, too. "I'll get the coffee," she said, accepting the role of assistant mediator in this strained mess of a marriage.

Seth finally found his voice. "Amy?" He gestured to the living room.

"Yeah. Okay." She rose and stalked into the living room. Seth followed.

Jackson stayed behind a moment. "How mad is she?"

"While she waited for me to get here she was researching divorce lawyers on the internet," she whispered. "Where was he?"

Jackson shook his head. "He hasn't said. I'm glad you're here." He leaned in and gave her a quick kiss on the lips.

Why didn't you call me? she wanted to snap, but thought maybe a guy not calling for one day rated pretty low on the scale compared to the fledgling marriage imploding in the other room.

She found a tray, a wedding gift probably being used for the first time, and put two fresh mugs on it. She filled them with fresh coffee and topped up hers and Amy's. When she opened the fridge, she found cartons of both milk and coffee cream. She poured some of each into two of the cream jugs. Amy seemed to have a lot of cream and sugar sets. She knew she was stalling for time. She did not want to face this. There was both white sugar and fancy Italian coffee sugar already in bowls, so she added those to the tray along with some silver coffee spoons. Jackson hefted the tray and they walked into the living room.

Amy had chosen to sit in one of the armchairs. Seth sat across from her on the couch.

By unspoken agreement, she took the chair beside her friend and Jackson placed the tray on the coffee table, then sat beside Seth.

She'd often heard the expression "you could cut the silence with a knife," but she thought this one needed a jackhammer.

She put the cream and fancy sugar into Amy's coffee since she knew exactly how she liked it. She even stirred the brew for her friend. She passed her the mug and patted her knee in support. She passed Jackson a mug, knowing he liked it black.

"Seth? Cream and sugar?"

"One cream. One sugar."

"Right." She felt as though she were putting on a one-woman show since she was the only one doing anything and the other three all seemed to be watching her.

She passed Seth his coffee. Took her own and sat back down beside Amy.

Finally, Seth said, "It's not what you think."

Amy replied, "Where the hell were you all night?"

While everyone stared at him, waiting for an answer, Seth grew red in the face and shuffled uncomfortably. One of his sports socks had slipped down his ankle. "I was sitting in my car, outside your old apartment. I fell asleep."

Whatever Lauren had been expecting, and admittedly the range was pretty narrow, she'd never imagined that.

Amy said, "You were doing what?"

Seth leaned forward and looked down at the floor. "I know it's stupid. I go there and look up at the window where you used to live. And I remember how it was before, you know."

"Before we got married?"

"Yeah."

"Before you promised in front of God and all our family and friends to love me forever?" Her voice was rising.

"Yeah."

Amy stood up. Her coffee wobbled precariously and she slammed it down, spilling dark liquid on the new tray. "Is that where you've been going? All those times you've disappeared on me?"

"No. Sometimes I go to my office and look back through old pictures of us."

"Oh, God," she cried. "I do that, too." And then she burst into tears. "It used to be so easy," Amy sobbed. "We were so in love. Why is marriage so hard?"

Jackson had been sitting watching the pair of newlyweds with a scornful expression on his face. Now it was he who rose and put his coffee down. "You talk about love as though it's a Disney movie. Love isn't like that. It's about caring about another person, even when you don't want to. It's about wanting them to be happy and have everything they ever wanted even if what they want isn't you."

Jackson wasn't looking at Amy when he said the words. He was looking right at Lauren, and at the expression in his eyes, her heart began to pound.

"That's easy for you to say," Seth countered. "You've never been in love."

"Yes," Jackson said. "I have."

"When? You never told me."

There was a tiny pause when she felt as though something rare and magical was happening. "I am," Jackson said. "I am in love with an amazing woman right now."

Seth snorted. "I bet she doesn't break your balls if you leave your socks on the floor, or you say something stupid."

He raised an eyebrow, and she felt that their path had been the opposite of Amy and Seth's. They'd had all their disagreements first. She knew all his weaknesses, had pinched at him for most of them, and he'd done the same for her.

"Oh, she lets me know all the time when I've said something stupid. She's not easy on me. Not at all. But she's the first person I think about when I wake up in the morning, the first person I want to tell when something funny or crazy or important happens. She's the last person I think about at night. The only woman I've ever known who's made me believe in love."

Only now did he break eye contact with Lauren and

turn to look at Seth and then Amy. "You can't give up. If you love each other, you have to fight for it."

"What do you think, Lauren?" Amy asked.

Lauren took a moment simply to savor this new knowledge that she was loved by the man she'd never believed could make her happy, and who seemed to be doing exactly that.

"I think," she said slowly, "that if we can spend more time appreciating the good in people we love than fixating on the bad, then we might be surprised at what we find."

"Sure, that sounds good," Amy said. "But try it in the real world." She glanced at each of them in turn, then back to Lauren. "Let's see you find the good in Jackson."

She acted as though she'd totally stumped Lauren, and Seth guffawed aloud. "Good one, honey."

"The good in Jackson," she said. She gazed at him and found him looking right at her, into her. "Jackson does a good job hiding all that is best about him so it's easy to think he's someone that he's not. Jackson is kind. I never knew that before, but he is. I thought he was a stuck-up rich boy, and he let me think that. But he's not. He's decent, hardworking, trustworthy, a good friend. He's funny, honorable, sexy, and there's something about him that makes me feel better when he's around."

As declarations went, she was putting herself right out there and it felt good. It felt right. All this time, they'd been falling in love in the shadows, not even realizing what was happening. Now that they were saying these things aloud they didn't seem so frightening.

It was Amy's turn to scoff. "Oh, come on. That

sounds fine, but you're not married to someone who doesn't treat you like a princess anymore."

Of course, Amy and Seth were so caught up in their own drama she didn't think either of them had figured out that two people who'd always thought they hated each other were declaring their love right in front of them. She smiled at Jackson, knowing he was thinking the same thing, and in return she got that crinkly-lidded smile that made her weak at the knees.

She turned to Amy. "No. And I don't want to be with someone who treats me like a princess. I want to be treated like an adult, an equal. Amy, so should you. Seth isn't on this earth to make you feel good about yourself. That's your job. Maybe your expectations are too high."

"You can say that again," Seth agreed, shooting a triumphant look at his wife as though he'd won a point in some game instead of fighting for his marriage.

"And you're as bad," she said, rounding on him. "Amy's a normal woman with needs. She's going to get PMS and bad hair days, and your job is to love her anyway. It's easy to love when everything's going well. It's when times get tough that you find out what you're made of." She sighed. "Times are tough for you two right now. Are you willing to fight for love? To fight for your marriage?"

"I don't want to lose Seth," Amy wailed.

"Good. That's a good start. How about you, Seth?"

"I still love her," he admitted, sounding less than happy about it.

"Okay. Look, I'm no marriage counselor and I really think you two should go visit one and get some guidance, but here's what I want you to do. Right in front of us, like you did when you got married. Seth, can you tell Amy why you fell in love with her?"

He fidgeted and scratched his knee. "You mean, now?"

She had no idea what she was doing, but they were both listening and she didn't think she could possibly make things worse, so she went with her instincts. "Yes, now."

"I don't know. I loved how sexy she was. Her amazing boobs. Her pretty smile."

That was about the most shallow reasoning Lauren had ever heard, and she was about to say so when Amy said, "Oh, Seth. Really? You really think I'm sexy?"

"You know I do."

"Okay, anything else?"

"I think she'll make a great mother. She's fun to be around. She's a good cook."

"How about you, Amy? What made you fall in love with Seth?"

She giggled. "I liked his shoulders. His big football-playing shoulders. And the way all the guys looked up to him. I could see he was a leader. I knew he'd take care of me."

"Oh, baby, you know I will. I'll always be here for you."

The two fell on each other, kissing noisily. "I'm so sorry," Amy said.

"No. It was me. My fault. I was an ass."

Jackson stepped forward, took her hand and said, "Okay, then. I think we should go."

The newlyweds didn't even hear them as they let themselves out of the house.

"Phew," she said, when the door shut behind them. "I hope they work it out. Do you think they will?"

"Right now, I'm not too worried about Seth and Amy. I have other things on my mind."

She glanced up, feeling suddenly shy. "Really? What kind of things?"

"You know, love and stuff."

She laughed, couldn't help it. "Love and stuff?"

He moved closer. "Like, could you? Do you?"

She could and she did, but she was a woman in love and she definitely deserved a real declaration. "No. No, no and no! You did better in there with an audience. This isn't how it's done, with 'will you' and 'could you.'"

"I've never told a woman I love her before," he said, running a hand through his hair. "It's huge. Terrifying."

"It is."

"Okay. Here goes." He shot her a glance. "You'll stop me if I'm wasting my time, right? You won't let me make a fool of myself for nothing?"

Oh, he was so adorable. She wanted to memorize every second, every expression that flitted across his face on this momentous morning. "You won't be wasting your time," she promised.

"I'm nervous."

"Me, too."

He took her hands. "You're the one who creates real things that last."

She gripped his hands right back. "You know what stained-glass work is? It's making art out of things that don't go together. Opposing colors, different elements, but you seal them together and something magical happens. Once the different pieces bond, they're together forever. Is that what you want?"

"More than anything. I love you, Lauren."

"I was hoping that was what you were getting at back there."

"I do. I love you and I want to be with you."

"Was that true? What you said in there?"

"About you being the first thing I think about when I wake up and the last thing I think about at night?"

She nodded.

"Yes. It is. And I edited out a few parts, like how the world feels right when I'm deep inside you, and when you're curled beside me in the night, our bodies touching, and how waking up beside you is the best part of the morning. I'm not perfect, and I don't think you're perfect. But I'm willing to work at it. More than anything, I want you to be happy."

"I want that for you, too. Oh, Jackson, I love you, too. So much. And it hit me so fast I never saw it coming."

"That's how it was for me, too." He looked deep into her eyes. "So, what do you say?"

"What, exactly, are you asking me?"

"Will you go to Amy and Seth's housewarming party with me on Saturday?"

She choked on a laugh. "You're asking me to a housewarming party?"

He put a hand to her hair, stroked down and cupped her cheek with his warm palm. "I am asking you to walk in, holding my hand, in public. In front of all our friends and the people we care about, we'll show up as a couple."

Her eyes widened as she realized exactly what he

was getting at. "They'll torment us. All those years that we hated each other, and now, to admit we're in love?"

He nodded. Grinning. "And Willy and the frat boys might even figure out that their wedding night prank actually worked."

"I have to think about this."

"Say yes. If we can face the mockery of our friends, we can do anything."

"You love me that much?"

"You have no idea."

"Then, yes."

He leaned in, kissed her slowly, sweetly, and suddenly she was being crushed in his arms. She couldn't get close enough.

Behind her she heard the townhouse door open. "Lauren? Jackson?" Amy squeaked. Then she yelled, "Seth, get out here. You're never going to believe this."

* * * * *

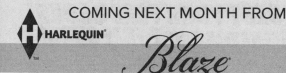
#855 ROLLING LIKE THUNDER
Thunder Mountain Brotherhood
by Vicki Lewis Thompson
Chelsea Trask might just be able to save the financially troubled
ranch Finn O'Roarke once called home—if the scorching
chemistry between her and the sexy brewmaster leaves them
any time to work at all!

#856 THE MIGHTY QUINNS: DEVIN
The Mighty Quinns
by Kate Hoffmann
When Elodie Winchester returns to her hometown, Sheriff
Devin Cassidy wants to reignite the passion between them,
even if it costs him everything he's worked for...and exposes a
shocking family secret.

#857 SEX, LIES AND DESIGNER SHOES
by Kimberly Van Meter
Rian Dalton likes to keep his business separate from pleasure.
Until he meets client CoCo Abelli, an heiress with a reckless
streak. Now Rian can't keep his hands to himself!

#858 A COWBOY RETURNS
Wild Western Heat
by Kelli Ireland
He's back. Eli Covington was Regan Matthews's first love—but not
the man she married. Working together to save his New Mexico
ranch brings up old feelings that are far too tempting to resist.

REQUEST YOUR FREE BOOKS!
2 FREE NOVELS PLUS 2 FREE GIFTS!

H HARLEQUIN®

Blaze®
red-hot reads!

YES! Please send me 2 FREE Harlequin® Blaze® novels and my 2 FREE gifts (gifts are worth about $10). After receiving them, if I don't wish to receive any more books, I can return the shipping statement marked "cancel." If I don't cancel, I will receive 4 brand-new novels every month and be billed just $4.74 per book in the U.S. or $5.21 per book in Canada. That's a savings of at least 14% off the cover price. It's quite a bargain. Shipping and handling is just 50¢ per book in the U.S. and 75¢ per book in Canada.* I understand that accepting the 2 free books and gifts places me under no obligation to buy anything. I can always return a shipment and cancel at any time. Even if I never buy another book, the two free books and gifts are mine to keep forever.

150/350 HDN GH2D

Name _____ (PLEASE PRINT) _____

Address _____ Apt. # _____

City _____ State/Prov. _____ Zip/Postal Code _____

Signature (if under 18, a parent or guardian must sign)

Mail to the **Reader Service:**
IN U.S.A.: P.O. Box 1867, Buffalo, NY 14240-1867
IN CANADA: P.O. Box 609, Fort Erie, Ontario L2A 5X3

Want to try two free books from another line?
Call 1-800-873-8635 or visit www.ReaderService.com.

* Terms and prices subject to change without notice. Prices do not include applicable taxes. Sales tax applicable in N.Y. Canadian residents will be charged applicable taxes. Offer not valid in Quebec. This offer is limited to one order per household. Not valid for current subscribers to Harlequin Blaze books. All orders subject to credit approval. Credit or debit balances in a customer's account(s) may be offset by any other outstanding balance owed by or to the customer. Please allow 4 to 6 weeks for delivery. Offer available while quantities last.

Your Privacy—The Reader Service is committed to protecting your privacy. Our Privacy Policy is available online at www.ReaderService.com or upon request from the Reader Service.

We make a portion of our mailing list available to reputable third parties that offer products we believe may interest you. If you prefer that we not exchange your name with third parties, or if you wish to clarify or modify your communication preferences, please visit us at www.ReaderService.com/consumerchoice or write to us at Reader Service Preference Service, P.O. Box 9062, Buffalo, NY 14240-9062. Include your complete name and address.

HB15

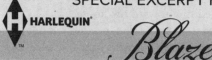
Elodie hurried downstairs and threw open the front door.
She stepped out into the storm, running across the lawn.
When she reached the police cruiser, she stopped. "What
are you doing out here?" she shouted above the wind.

Dev slowly got out of the car, his hand braced along the
top of the door. "I couldn't sleep."

"I couldn't, either," she shouted.

It was all he needed. He stepped toward her and before
she knew it, she was in his arms, his hands smoothing over
the rain-soaked fabric of her dress. His lips covered hers in
a desperate, deeply powerful kiss. He molded her mouth to
his, still searching for something even more intimate.

The fabric of her dress clung to her naked skin, a feeble
barrier to his touch. Elodie fought the urge to reach for the
hem of her dress and pull it over her head. They were on a
public street, with houses all around.

"Come with me," she murmured. She laced her fingers through his and pulled him toward the house.

Once they reached the protection of the veranda, he grabbed her waist again, pulling her into another kiss. Dev smoothed his hand up her torso until he found her breast and he cupped it, his thumb teasing at her taut nipple.

Elodie reached for the hem of his shirt, but it was tucked underneath his leather utility belt. "Take this off," she murmured, frantically searching for the buckle.

He carefully unclipped his gun and set it on a nearby table. A moment later, his utility belt dropped to the ground, followed by his badge and, finally, his shirt. Her palms skimmed over hard muscle and smooth skin. His shoulders, once slight, were now broad, his torso a perfect V.

Dev reached for the hem of her dress and bunched it in his fists, pulling it higher and higher until it was twisted around her waist. He gently pushed her back against the door and she moaned as his fingertips skimmed the soft skin of her inner thigh.

Wild sensations raced through her body and she trembled as she anticipated what would come next…

Don't miss
THE MIGHTY QUINNS: DEVIN by Kate Hoffmann,
available August 2015 wherever
Harlequin® Blaze® books and ebooks are sold.

www.Harlequin.com

HBEXPO715

JUST CAN'T GET ENOUGH?

Join our social communities
and talk to us online.

You will have access to the latest
news on upcoming titles and special
promotions, but most importantly,
you can talk to other fans about your
favorite Harlequin reads.

Harlequin.com/Community

Facebook.com/HarlequinBooks

Twitter.com/HarlequinBooks

Pinterest.com/HarlequinBooks

HARLEQUIN®

A *Romance* FOR EVERY MOOD™

Stay up-to-date on all your
romance-reading news with the
Harlequin Shopping Guide,
featuring bestselling authors, exciting new
miniseries, books to watch and more!

The newest issue will be delivered right to you
with our compliments! There are 4 each year.

Signing up is easy.

EMAIL

ShoppingGuide@Harlequin.ca

WRITE TO US

HARLEQUIN BOOKS
Attention: Customer Service Department
P.O. Box 9057, Buffalo, NY 14269-9057

OR PHONE

1-800-873-8635 in the United States
1-888-343-9777 in Canada

Please allow 4-6 weeks for delivery of the first issue by mail.